I SHOT THE SHERIFF

DEBORAH WALLACE

Deborah Wallace

I Shot the Sheriff

Published by Deborah Wallace

Copyright © 2019 by Deborah Wallace

ISBN: 978-1-951457-05-1

Cover Art by Raymond and Deborah Wallace
Photographs by:
Couple: Alvin Mahmudov
Cabin: Viktor Talashuk

About This Book

The story idea for this book came to me on a LONG lonely drive to Michigan from Massachusetts. I'd taken a stack of CDs to listen to since a radio is unreliable on a six-hundred mile trip. I was listening to *I Shot the Sheriff* by Eric Clapton and imagining what would cause someone to shoot the sheriff and protest that he hadn't shot the deputy, which meant someone *had* shot the deputy. I hope you enjoy my version of how it may have happened.

Chapter 1

Claire Dickens had no idea why she'd accepted her ex-husband's invitation to dinner so he could bounce ideas off her. He'd done it when they were married. Jeffery should have asked Brad. As a police detective, he worked on cases all the time and was good at it. He was Jeffery's best friend. But Jeffery had convinced her she was the only one who could help him. She'd always enjoyed listening to him talk about his day and fitting facts together like a puzzle. That was why he'd never tried to make detective. He couldn't do it himself. His superiors knew his weaknesses and wouldn't have assigned him a difficult case.

She turned into the parking lot of her favorite restaurant. The first letter of the neon sign beside the door was dark, leaving it to read *aptain's Net*. The long, low stucco building had stood on this corner for as long as she could remember, although, when she was a child, it had been a small grocery store.

She hoped Jeffery would keep this dinner on topic and not try again to get back with her. He should have given up by now in thinking it would help his cause to tell her over and over he didn't remember going to bed with that woman. Her breath left in a huff. Maybe she shouldn't have agreed to come.

It was late enough, even for a Friday, that there weren't many cars in the parking lot. She had her choice of empty spaces. She backed into a space, so she could watch for his car, and cracked the window open. The scent of fried fish drifted in. His car wasn't there yet and she tapped her fingers on the steering wheel, then flipped the visor down and checked her make-up one last time in the mirror. She ran a hand over her dark hair. A crease marred the space between her eyebrows and she raised them to smooth it, sighing.

Maybe he'd changed his mind and not told her, but he'd never stood her up before without a call. Something had delayed him.

His gold Highlander barreled into the lot. She checked her watch. Seven minutes late. He was always early. He couldn't have changed that much in eight months. After parking in his favorite spot on the other side of the lot, he got out and headed her way. She stepped out and waited beside her car. Since he asked her there, let him be the one to cover the distance between them. He still had a self-assurance about him, especially with his muscles filling out his deputy uniform. She melted just a bit, but steeled herself against it.

His gaze darted around the parking lot, back and around again. Prickles skittered up her spine. Maybe he wasn't as self-assured as she thought.

By the time he reached her, *she* was searching the parking lot. For what, she didn't know. "So, what's this about?"

He towered over her, but even now it made her feel safe.

He ran a hand over his forehead, and through his short blond hair. His shoulders were tense. If they'd still been married, she'd promise to massage them when they got home. She mentally shook herself. Never going to happen.

"I'm in trouble and you're the only one I trust. You see through the unimportant details, leaving what matters."

"What about Brad? Why aren't you asking him for help? What kind of trouble?"

He took her arm, but she resisted. He searched the parking lot again. A car drove by and he jerked his head to follow it. That frightened her. He appeared nervous and

Jeffery was never nervous.

He cleared his throat and tugged on her arm. "Let's go inside."

She wrenched her arm away. "Why haven't you asked Brad for help?"

"We'll discuss it inside." His voice was firm, not to be argued with.

They'd only marched a few steps when Sheriff Dean Crowley's giant SUV swung into the parking lot, blocking the path to the door. She'd never cared for Dean, but this was going too far. Jeffery sidestepped as Crowley hauled his bulky body out of the cruiser and stood beside the open door, the vehicle still running. She gave Jeffery a puzzled expression. His pulse beat a fast pace on the side of his neck and he lifted his chin before shoving her behind him.

His vice-like grip on her arm prevented her from tugging free. "Jeffery, what are you doing?"

"Claire, stay behind me. Please." His firm voice pleaded and his grip tightened.

Was the sheriff part of whatever this was? She peeked over Jeffery's tense shoulder. Why did he need to protect her from the sheriff? *Jeffery, what have you done?*

Crowley's car blocked anyone from seeing them from the restaurant door. A quick glance around the parking lot showed no one else was outside. She gasped when she focused back on Crowley and the gun pointed at Jeffery's chest. No, this couldn't be happening. There was no reason for the sheriff to hold a gun on his own deputy. His face hardened, his gray eyebrows pulled down behind his wire-framed glasses. No fake friendliness this time.

"Dean, she doesn't know anything. Leave her out of it."

"It's too late, Dickens. I overheard you inviting her help, so she already knows too much."

Jeffery yanked his gun from the holster on his hip, but

before he could level it, a quiet shot jerked him back. He toppled over, trapping her under his heavy weight. The sheriff did not shoot Jeffery. But he had and she'd been dropped into a nightmare.

She struggled to free herself from the dead weight on top of her. No! Don't think that. She managed a few quick, shallow breaths. Crowley's hard soled shoes clicked closer and closer. Did he plan to shoot her, too? He'd have to. He hadn't warned Jeffery to put his hands up, so he didn't have a valid reason to shoot him. Something was very, very wrong. Time was running out. She worked at slowing her breathing, reaching for an inner calm, so she could think.

Her gun was in her purse, trapped between them. She couldn't open the flap to get it. Jeffery and Brad had both insisted she learn how to use a gun and carry it, both worried that as a reporter she might get into a sticky situation. And the only time she ever needed a gun, she couldn't open her purse. Jeffery's gun. He'd pulled it out. There. On the ground beside her. She snatched it to her side, and hoped Crowley hadn't seen her collect it.

The sheriff stopped beside her shoulder. "I was surprised to see you two together, Claire. I thought I had succeeded in breaking you up."

"What are you talking about?" Her hand shook as she made sure the safety was off and put her finger on the trigger. She wasn't sure if she'd be able to aim or fire.

The sheriff's foot shoved Jeffery's shoulder, partially revealing her, leaving him off balance. His gun pointed at her for only a second before she shot him. He stumbled back and fell. She froze. What had she done? She dragged in a breath. She'd done what she needed to do in order to survive.

People would hear the shot. Hers wasn't silenced. She had to get as far away as she could. She didn't know what Jeffery was involved in, but she was in danger now. If the sheriff couldn't be trusted, she couldn't trust anyone. She dropped the gun and thrust Jeffery with panicked strength and freed herself.

She couldn't hold back the tears when all life left his eyes.

"Jeffery, no. You can't do this. Don't be dead. Not like this." She checked for a pulse and didn't find one.

A car drove into the lot and she whipped her head around. The familiar squeak of *Captain's Net*'s door opening spurred her into motion. How could anyone believe her when she hardly believed what happened? She blinked the tears away, and racing to her car, jumped in and tore out of the space. Giving a last glance in her rear view mirror, she sped from the parking lot.

****

At the end of the quarter mile drive, Claire parked her car behind the cabin Jeffery's Uncle Derrick had left him. She held her breath as she slid her key into the back door lock, and let it out when it turned. Jeffery hadn't changed it. She closed the door with a soft click and leaned against it, letting her shoulders drop.

Jeffery was dead. Shot in front of her. He didn't deserve that. She'd known him most of her life and couldn't believe he was gone. Months ago, she'd accepted he wouldn't be a part of her life anymore, but at least she'd known he was around somewhere.

She pushed away from the door, closed the dark drapes, lit a kerosene lantern and set it on the floor. Its soft glow would give her dim light without brightening the windows with the electric lamps.

She paced the rustic living room, past the faded couch to the small table beside the front door, around the small island in the kitchen, past the kitchen table and back to the couch. Three doors lined the wall opposite the front door, two bedrooms with a miniscule bathroom between them. Derrick had installed it when she was ten. Before that, they'd had an outhouse and no shower, so she didn't mind the claustrophobic room.

A small bookcase across from the couch held Derrick's favorite paperbacks. She ran her finger across a thick layer of dust on the top, and swiped it on her pants. If she was here long enough, she'd have to clean. The last time it had been done was probably her last time there.

For once, she wished the cabin had a TV or radio. Uncle Derrick had always said they were spending time there to get away from those kinds of distractions, and do things together. She loved those many weekends and summer weeks spent at the cabin. She wished she could go back to when they were kids. Her only concern had been if she could do everything Jeffery and Brad could. Who could catch the biggest or most fish? Who could reach the top of the hill first? Never her. Who could swim under water the longest or reach a particular rock first? There were so many competitions Derrick set up for them, but he never made it into a real competition. He wanted them to best themselves. He kept them out of trouble.

After nearly an hour, she calmed enough to sit, and groaned when her bruised tailbone screamed. She leaned back on the old, dusty couch with care, and stared up at the dark rafters. She shivered when she realized the bullet that killed Jeffery could have gone through him and killed her, too. He got her into this mess, but he saved her life, too. And now there was probably an all points bulletin out for her arrest for killing the sheriff.

She covered her eyes with the crook of her elbow and concentrated on remembering every word Jeffery had said on the phone and in the parking lot, but none of it explained why Dean Crowley would shoot him. He'd left too much unsaid. Jeffery had it right—she didn't know anything.

Claire tensed at a knock on the door. How long had she been here? A couple of hours?

"Claire, I know you're in there." Brad's angry voice grabbed her through the door.

She stared at the door, panic churning in her belly. She wasn't surprised Brad thought to check for her at the cabin. Where else could she have gone? She dragged her feet across the room, released the lock and pulled the doorknob.

He forced his way in and glared at her for several seconds with his clear blue eyes. His brown hair was mussed where he would have run his hand through it. And did it again. He stretched up to his full six foot two height and stared at the ceiling before glaring down at her. "I heard at the station. You killed Jeffery?"

"No!" He couldn't believe that. "The sheriff shot him and then he tried to shoot me." She silently begged for him to trust her.

Brad leaned forward and scrutinized Claire's face, as if trying to figure out if she told the truth. Had she ever lied to him?

"That's not what Crowley said."

"He's alive?" It was probably a good thing. She didn't want to be a killer, even in self-defense.

"Yeah. He said he was turning into the parking lot when you yelled at Jeffery, and then the two of you were struggling. He heard a shot and Jeffery fell. He jumped out of the car and you stood over Jeffery. A gun was on the ground on the opposite side of him. He said it appeared Jeffery was trying to wrestle it away from you when it went off. Then you saw him, leaned down and yanked out Jeffery's service revolver, and shot him."

"That's not what happened!" She blinked back the tears threatening to escape. "What he said doesn't even make sense." Anger simmered in her voice. "I may have divorced Jeffery, but I couldn't hate him. You know how close we've always been."

Brad stared at her with his hands on his hips, and took a deep breath, visibly containing his anger. He pointed to the couch. "Okay. Let's sit down."

They sat only inches apart, but it may as well have been a canyon between them.

"Start at the beginning. Tell me what happened."

She filled her lungs. She was a reporter. How many times had she blocked her emotions to do her work? Do it now or be arrested for murder.

She studied her intertwined hands. "Jeffery called me this afternoon and said he wanted to run something by me. He said I was always helpful when he was working on a tough case, and he was having trouble figuring something out. So, I agreed to meet him."

"What did he want to discuss?" His voice had calmed.

She didn't know if he would believe her, but at least he was listening.

"He wouldn't tell me over the phone. And we didn't get a chance to talk at *Captain's Net*." She pounded her fist on the couch, raising a cloud of dust. She needed to vacuum the furniture. An hysterical giggle nearly escaped, but she held it in. She'd rather be cleaning the cabin top to bottom than discussing Jeffery's death.

"We'd both gotten to the *Net* and were headed inside. Jeffery seemed nervous. Dean showed up and pulled a gun on us."

He frowned. "Was it his service revolver?"

She shrugged. "Jeffery shoved me behind him, so I didn't actually see him take it out." She closed her eyes and

8

let her mind wind through the events from earlier that evening. From the ground, she'd seen the gun in his hand, but his hip holster had a gun, too. "No. I didn't notice at the time, but there was a gun in his holster." She gaped at Brad in surprise.

"Well, that explains why his revolver wasn't fired. It also makes it seem like you're the only one who fired."

"Me?" she squeaked.

"Continue your story." He placed his hand over hers, but snatched it back.

The momentary warmth made her realize how the cold had penetrated into her soul.

Did he believe her so far? They'd been friends for twenty years. That had to count for something. He'd have to know she wouldn't shoot Jeffery.

She explained her ordeal. She'd never thought about how witnesses relived the trauma. It became real all over again when she told him, the images playing in her head. She wrapped her hands around her arms to control the shivers. Jeffery was dead. Maybe it was all a bad dream. She wished it was.

"What you say doesn't make any more sense than what Crowley said. The sheriff shot his deputy?"

She raised her voice and slapped her hand on the cushion beside her, having forgotten about the dust. "At least it's the truth! There were two guns fired at the scene. Why would I use two guns? And have a third in my purse, unfired. This must have had something to do with whatever Jeffery wanted to talk about."

"Claire, calm down." He rested his hand on her arm. "I didn't say *I* didn't believe you, but no one else is going to."

She picked up her purse from the floor. Opening it, she tipped it so he could see inside. "See. My gun is still there. Why would I have two?"

"Crowley could say you didn't want to incriminate yourself."

She glared at him. "And if I'd wanted to shoot Jeffery, I'd have done it months ago and in a more secluded spot than a restaurant parking lot." She pointed a finger at him. "And what about the trajectory of the bullet? I shot Crowley from flat on my back. It would have been a different angle face to face."

"Good point. I'll have to check into that. What did Crowley say?"

She took a breath and rubbed her forehead. "It all happened so fast. Let me think." She stared into the dead eyes of a moose head on the wall. As dead as Jeffery's were. She blinked back tears. "He told Jeffery he shouldn't have involved me. Jeffery begged him to leave me out of it, but then Dean shot him. As he walked toward us, he said he was surprised to see us together." Pain twisted her heart, and her eyes widened. "He said he thought he had succeeded in breaking us up."

She couldn't hold back her tears. "All along Jeffery said he couldn't remember how he ended up in bed with that woman, and I just thought he was too drunk to remember. But he never drank so much he got drunk. The sheriff must have drugged him. And the anonymous call I got for an interview on my investigation was a setup for me to find them. I was so upset I didn't even think about how I got there."

He wrapped an arm around her shoulder and leaned his head against the top of her head. "Claire—"

"No. All I could think about when I saw them together was my mother had taken my dad back time after time when he cheated on her, and I wasn't going to be like her. I knew Jeffery wasn't like that. I should have listened."

She wept. All the lost time where they both had suffered.

If only she'd trusted him enough to question the circumstances. Her reporter instincts should have warned her that she'd been set up to find his infidelity. Instead, the instinct that had kicked in was the one to protect her heart from repeated pain.

He ran his hand up and down her back. Many minutes passed before she recovered, rummaged through her purse and found a tissue. She dried her face and blew her nose.

"I'm sorry. I didn't mean to fall apart." She blinked to clear her eyes and worked up a trembling smile. "And I'm sorry I got your shirt all wet." She ran her fingers over the damp spot.

Brad caressed her hand. "You've had a tough evening."

Fresh tears trickled down her cheeks. "You have, too. You lost your best friend."

Claire wiped her cheeks again. "Why didn't Jeffery talk to you about whatever he's been investigating? I asked him, but he said he'd tell me inside."

"That's a question I don't have an answer to. And I have no idea how I'm going to find out."

He ran a hand through his hair. "How are we going to investigate while keeping you hidden? It might not take them long to find Jeffery owned this cabin."

She grabbed his forearm. "Brad, if I'm arrested, I don't think I'll live to be questioned. Dean will find a way to get rid of me. If I get a chance to tell my version of what happened, they'll have to investigate Sheriff Crowley, and I don't think he wants anyone inspecting his life." She flopped back against the couch. "I can't believe I'm talking like this."

"I wonder if Jeffery realized he was risking your life when he set up the meeting to talk to you."

"He probably thought he had more time." Claire jerked up. "Brad! We have to get Jeffery's laptop before it gets taken for evidence. If he's got anything about his

11

investigation on it, someone's going to wipe it."

"I hadn't thought of that. Why don't I swing by there on my way home? I'll have to break in."

"I still have a key." Claire dug into the bottom of her purse and grabbed a key ring. "Here." She dropped it in his hand. "The bigger one unlocks the house doors. The smaller one's for the shed."

Brad stood, and took her hand. "Stay here. I'll bring the laptop and food tomorrow. We'll figure out our game plan then."

Claire gave him a hug, and gazed up at him. "Thank you for believing me and helping."

"We've been friends too long for me to do anything else."

It paid to have a police detective for a best friend.

Chapter 2

Brad drove past Jeffery's ranch style house. The bushes in front of the house were too low to hide anyone unless they crouched. All the windows were dark, and no police car stood in front of it. They could have been and gone already. He'd find out once he got inside if Jeffery's laptop was still there.

He parked a block away, strolled back as if he lived in the neighborhood, keeping his gaze moving. At nearly midnight, the street was empty. No one peeked out windows. He arrived at the yard, and stepped against the bushes bordering the property, waiting, his heart pounding. A dog barked a couple of yards away. Maybe he'd spooked it.

A streetlight at each corner fell short of the house in the middle of the block. The crescent moon gave little additional light. The backyard was more dark than shadowed. Once he stood behind the small shed in the back, he paused and scanned the house again.

He'd been surprised when Jeffery had kept the house after Claire divorced him. They'd had a lot of happy memories there, and he didn't know how Jeffery could live with that. But Jeffery had held onto the hope that Claire would return.

Brad extracted the key from his pocket. He wasn't breaking in, but he shouldn't enter the house of a murder victim. He took several deep breaths to calm himself before cutting across the empty expanse to the house. He set each foot with care on the wooden steps, winced and paused when

13

the second one squeaked. Finally at the back door, he let himself in, locking the door behind him.

He'd been in the house many times in the four years Jeffery had owned it, so didn't need his flashlight to find the office. Dim light showed through the wide window in the living room, enough to outline the doorway. His hands skimmed the kitchen island and the doorframe, turning left to head toward the bedrooms.

He stepped into the office on his left and flicked on his flashlight. The windows overlooked the backyard, so he wouldn't have to worry about anyone seeing flashes of light from the street. Keeping the light low, he skimmed the room, stopping on the empty spot where Claire's desk used to sit.

The laptop sat on Jeffery's desk, plugged in to charge. He unplugged the cord, wound it up and stuffed it into his pocket. As he picked it up, he remembered Jeffery sometimes kept files on a flash drive. He slid open the desk drawer and shone the light in as he nudged pens and sticky pads out of the way. He found two drives and added them to his pocket, then slid the drawer closed.

The back step squeaked and his head jerked up. He snatched up the laptop, turned off his light and shoved it in his pocket. He stepped into the closet and dragged the door closed, turning the knob to silence the latch. His heart pounded. Had they seen his light? It couldn't be the police. They'd come in the front. If whoever this was found him, would they try to kill him? This had to be about more than Sheriff Crowley.

The back door opened and quick footsteps stalked through the kitchen. A man's heavier step. Light under the closet door preceded the steps into the office.

He took in shallow breaths and hoped the guy couldn't hear his heart pounding and wouldn't check the closet. His hand touched his gun for reassurance, ready to pull it out if the door opened. If that happened, he hoped he didn't end up pointing it at someone he knew. He strained to hear anything that would give the intruder away—breathing, a brush of clothing—but only footsteps filled the silence. Desk drawers opened and closed and footsteps left the room. He took a slow breath and relaxed his shoulders.

Drawers opened and closed in Jeffery's bedroom across the hall and then there was rummaging in drawers in the guest room beside the office.

The back door closed, the step squeaked and he waited, straining to hear any other sounds. After several minutes of silence, he nudged the door open and waited a minute more.

Where else should he search? If there was anything to find in the bedrooms, the intruder had taken it. The only place left was the basement. He'd helped Jeffery finish off a room in the basement for a pool table. They'd set up a bar and small refrigerator. Jeffery had added a widescreen TV and overstuffed couch for times Claire didn't want to watch a game with them. She called it their man cave.

The closed hallway door led to the basement. One step down, he stopped, waiting for any betraying sound of someone below. Silence greeted him and he made his way down the stairs, turning on his flashlight at the bottom. The room appeared the same as the last time he'd seen it.

The TV, straight ahead, mounted on the wall, with Jeffery's weight bench and free weights tucked in the corner to the right. He turned left, scanned his flashlight over boxes against the wall. He opened the flap of one and found a red hairbrush, knickknacks, a couple of books, and women's clothing. Claire must have left behind a few items and Jeffery hadn't had the heart to get rid of them. He sighed. His friend had been devastated when Claire left.

Through a doorway, he approached the washer and dryer with cabinets overtop. He jerked open the cabinet doors. The usual laundry supplies and a stack of serving dishes filled the space. He tucked the flashlight into his pocket as he stretched to the back of the second shelf and ran his hand from corner to corner. Then he stepped over to the next cabinet and did the same, finding nothing but a screwdriver, hammer and paint brush.

Back in the main room, his light slid across the pool table. Brad stared, memories flashed through his head of long nights playing pool with Jeffery and sometimes Claire, too. They laughed and talked, drank beer and challenged each other to game after game. He smiled when he remembered that after Jeffery bought the pool table, Claire admitted to playing for hours to improve her skills. She'd always had the need to challenge them and worked hard to win. Jeffery took to distracting her during crucial shots. He would duck down across from her, so she'd have to look at him or he'd offer her his beer as she lined up her shot.

It would never happen again. His best friend was gone. No more games of pool, cheering football games together or going out to a bar. No more weekends at the cabin or hiking. His heart ached and he squeezed his eyes closed. There was never a time he didn't have Jeffery's friendship.

He willed his breathing to slow, and rubbed his eyes. He needed to find out for Jeffery why Crowley had killed him. And prove it *was* Crowley who killed Jeffery. For Claire. And for Jeffery. His friend would never forgive him if he didn't protect Claire.

His gaze still on the pool table, he remembered watching a movie with Jeffery where someone had hidden something on the bottom side of a pool table. Jeffery had glanced at his table and said if he needed to hide anything, that would be the place to do it. Would Jeffery remember? He set the laptop on the table and crouched down. Twisting, he stuck his head under and flashed his light at the underside of the table. Pay dirt! He grabbed the business size envelope, stuck with two pieces of masking tape, and slid it into his jacket pocket. He stood, picked up the laptop and headed for the stairs.

He pocketed the flashlight, made his way through the kitchen, scanned the backyard through the window. No movement. He opened the door enough to slip through, paused, checking the yard again. He locked the door and worked his way back to his car the same way he'd come.

His gaze flicked to the rear view mirror every few seconds as he drove, taking a convoluted route home, and slipped into the garage, closing the door. He sagged in the seat. This was nothing like when he did surveillance or legal searches. He didn't like having to worry about being caught by the police or a criminal.

He picked up the laptop, and got out of the car. In the kitchen, he set it down on a small catch-all table to take off his jacket and hung it on a hook by the door. His hand dropped to the laptop. He'd do some poking around before going to bed.

"I'll take that laptop," a menacing voice said behind him.

His heart pounded as he swung around.

A gun pointed at his chest. He'd had guns pointed at him before, but it had always been in the line of duty, and his mindset expected the danger and automatically ticked through various courses of action. In his own home, he'd been caught unprepared. Time to get into work mode.

"What are you doing in my house?" He didn't recognize the short, muscular man in front of him. How did he get in and who sent him? Was he the man who'd been in Jeffery's house? He knew all the policemen at the station, at least by sight, and this man wasn't serving a search warrant.

"I came to collect the laptop." He nodded toward it. "So, back away from the table."

Brad's hand tightened around the edge of the laptop. The man could still shoot him after he stepped away. No good reason to leave a witness alive. Brad's chance of attacking before getting shot was pretty slim. And if he died here, would Claire be accused of killing him, too? He turned his foot toward the gunman.

"I wouldn't do that if I were you. I'm far enough away that you can't kick this." He wiggled the gun. "But I'm close enough to hit you without even trying. I don't mind leaving you dead."

With a burst of speed, Brad picked up the laptop. "All right. There's probably nothing important on it anyway." He threw it at the man's head. His gun pointed up while catching it and Brad tackled the guy, who grunted as they crashed to the floor. Brad slammed their hands to the tiled floor twice and yanked the gun free. He flung it across the room then punched the intruder in the jaw.

The guy swung and hit Brad on the side of the head. Pain exploded in his temple and he swayed, giving the man a chance to shove Brad off, turn and stumble to his feet. Brad stretched and caught the man's pant leg, but he yanked it away. Brad surged to his feet as the stranger threw open the front door.

"I didn't get paid enough for this."

Brad stopped at the door, watching the man flee. He slammed the door closed, locked the knob and the deadbolt. Both had been locked that morning. From the kitchen, he grabbed a chair a forced it under the doorknob, then did the same to the back door.

He ran upstairs and grabbed a duffle bag from his closet, stuffed clothes into it. He snatched it up and ran to his office where he grabbed his laptop and shoved it into the side pocket. Back downstairs, he picked up Jeffery's laptop and his jacket. He hit the garage door button as he passed into the garage and jumped into his car.

Brad started the car, and tapped his fingers on the steering wheel as the door took too long to rise. It couldn't be slower than normal, but it felt like agonizing minutes. He ran both hands through his hair and held the back of his neck, massaging the tightness out of his shoulders.

He hit the gas pedal, tires squealing, and clicked the button on the visor to reverse the door and raced out of the driveway. He drove three blocks, took a right and rolled to the curb. He needed a plan.

He couldn't call the police about the break in. They'd take Jeffery's laptop, and maybe arrest him for tampering with evidence. And what if Sheriff Crowley wasn't the only dirty cop at the station and they happened to send that person? He didn't know who to trust.

Is that why Jeffery had kept this a secret? He couldn't trust anyone? Including Brad? Or had he thought he'd be risking Brad's life, too? But then he'd risked Claire's.

Had someone followed him and he'd missed it? Did someone know Brad would go to Jeffery's house and figured they'd let him find what there was to find and then take it from him?

He wished Jeffery had asked for his help. Both Claire's and his lives were at stake now, so someone could keep this secret.

He pulled his cell phone out of his pocket and checked for messages. There were none. He turned it off, took out the battery and tossed them into the glove compartment.

Brad drove to his bank, and circled the building to reach the ATM in back. He stopped at the screen and shoved his card in the slot, punched in his PIN and his withdrawal request. He repeated until he had accumulated a thousand dollars.

After making a stop at the all night combo

grocery/department store at the edge of town for food, clothing for Claire and cell phones, he bypassed the cabin's road. He u-turned on a side road and waited five minutes to make sure he wasn't followed. Then he headed back to the correct road and past the driveway, reversing into the next drive, and killed the lights. He was far enough away he wouldn't be noticed, but close enough to see headlights come up the road. As he waited, he programmed each prepaid phone he'd purchased with the other's number.

He hoped no one had figured out yet that Claire could be hiding at Jeffery's cabin. Only family and close friends were aware he'd inherited it. Hopefully, they didn't tell the wrong people.

He was going to spend the night with Claire. Well, not *with* her, but at the cabin. The last time that happened they must have been eighteen. Derrick had noticed Claire and Jeffery were dating. He set Brad as an unofficial chaperone in the bedroom the three of them shared. Claire had the bottom bunk of one set of beds, and Jeffery the top and Brad the bottom of the other. His job was to make sure Jeffery stayed in his own bed. He grinned. There was never a problem with that. Jeffery wouldn't have dared to try anything with Derrick nearby.

After five minutes of no traffic, he headed back to the cabin and parked behind it. He picked up Jeffery's laptop and the bag of clothing, stepped up to the back door and gave a quiet knock. When he couldn't hear anything, he knocked harder and said, "Claire, it's me."

Footsteps approached the door.

"Brad?"

"Yes, let me in."

She opened the door and stifled a yawn. "What are you doing here?"

He set everything on the kitchen table. "I bought you

some clothes. I hope the sizes are okay."

He turned, but couldn't speak for a few seconds. She had found an old football jersey to wear. He didn't think she had anything on under it, and a long expanse of legs was on display. His breath caught in his throat, and his voice rasped. "I have to get the rest of the stuff."

He stepped outside, and sucked in deep breaths of cool, night air, steeling himself for returning to Claire. He'd keep his eyes on her face or they'd both be in trouble. He got the groceries from the backseat of his truck and brought them into the kitchen, turned on the refrigerator and stowed the perishables while she stood with her arms crossed on her chest. Probably protecting herself from his leer.

He closed the refrigerator door, braced himself, and faced her.

"Now—" Her eyes widened, and she touched a bruise on his jaw. "What happened?"

He gave her a brief rundown of the break-in at Jeffery's and the man waiting for him at his house. At her horrified expression, he waved a hand at his face. "Hey, other than this, I came back in one piece."

"But, he could have killed you."

"I was smarter than him." He wouldn't tell her how close it was.

He removed a cell phone from the shopping bag, and set it on the table. "Here's your new phone. I need to take your other phone for a ride."

"My phone!" She hurried to the couch, and rummaged through her purse, found the device and handed it over. "I didn't even think about the GPS in it. I'm such a muddled mess."

He gave her shoulder a squeeze. "Why don't you give me the cabin key? You can go back to sleep and I'll let myself in. We'll talk in the morning."

"But why are—" She yawned. "All right. All right. But first thing in the morning, you're telling me everything."

As he headed to the door, he hoped no one had thought yet to track Claire's phone.

Chapter 3

Claire woke to the savory scents of bacon and coffee. She stretched and froze. She'd lived alone for months. The only time she smelled coffee before she got out of bed was when she remembered to set the coffee pot up and turn on the timer. Opening her eyes, she stared at the beams in the bedroom. The events of the night before rushed back. Jeffery was dead and the police thought she'd murdered him. Brad was here to help her. He believed her.

When had he come in? He'd gotten less sleep than she had. He didn't use to be a morning person. Quite often, through their years at the cabin, he'd been the last to get up.

She rose and entered the tiny bathroom, speed showered and dried off, then realized the clothes Brad had bought for her still sat in the kitchen. She wrapped the towel around herself, wishing it were a bit wider. On second thought, it would be better to put the football jersey back on. Hopefully, the bag wasn't sitting on the floor, since the jersey wasn't much longer than the towel.

His back was to her when she opened the door. She snuck to the table and grabbed the bag as Brad peeked over his shoulder.

He swallowed and rasped out, "Morning, Claire."

She stopped, staring at his face.

He dropped his eyes to her breasts, then trailed down the too thin jersey, paused at the hem and traveled to her feet before they jumped back to her eyes, one corner of his mouth tipped up. He licked his lips.

She broke eye contact, snatched the bag, and fled to the bedroom. She closed the door and leaned against it, trying to catch her breath.

He'd never stared at her like that before, like he wanted to pick her up and carry her to bed. Her heartbeat quickened. Maybe she'd misinterpreted. He couldn't think about her that way. She'd been married to Jeffery and they'd been friends forever.

A shiver passed through her. No, it couldn't happen. Her ex-husband had been murdered, ripped from her life. She needed Brad to be her friend. Now, after she dressed, she had to go back into the kitchen, and pretend she hadn't noticed a thing.

****

His gaze followed her long, graceful legs until she disappeared behind the door.

He ran a hand through his hair. "Down, boy." What just happened? Sure, back when the three of them were teens, he'd been interested in Claire. Then Jeffery and Claire started dating and he blocked those feelings out. Obviously, they were still there and maybe even stronger than before. It was like a gate opened when Jeffery died, but it was too soon. They needed time to adjust to Jeffery being gone. It was wrong to want Claire right now.

He drew in a measured breath and let it out. A murder charge needed to be cleared and everything Jeffery had been involved in. There was too much they needed to find out before he should think of Claire as anything but a dear friend.

The bedroom door creaked open as he loaded their plates with bacon, eggs and toast. He picked them up, and smiled at her oversized shirt and pants. Which was probably a good thing. He needed to help Claire, not get into those pants.

"Morning." Her eyes darted away. "Thanks for the clothes."

"Sorry I didn't get the size right, but you look great in anything."

She rolled her eyes. "It's better than putting on yesterday's bloody clothes." She shivered. "Do you think there's any way I can get into my apartment to get more clothes?"

"They'll be watching it. I don't think *I* can get in either. Sorry."

She shrugged and sat down, stared at the empty table in front of her. Brad set the plates on the table. He replenished his cup of coffee, poured one for her, taking his time setting the old percolator back on the stove. He could do this. He and Claire were friends, had been for as long as he could remember. He wouldn't ruin it by taking it somewhere she might not want it to go.

He set her cup on the table and dropped into the chair opposite her, taking a drink from his own. While they ate, he told her what had happened the night before at Jeffery's and his houses.

He speared a piece of egg. "I'm glad it's Saturday. At least we can start going through what we have and maybe figure something out. Come Monday morning, I'll have to show up at the station."

He had no idea what he'd find when he got to work. Someone would ask if he knew where Claire was and he'd have to prepare to lie. Most would expect him to believe she'd killed his best friend. He wanted to defend her, but it would give himself away. He couldn't disagree with Sheriff Crowley's account of Jeffery's murder without the others realizing he'd talked to Claire.

After they'd finished eating, they cleared the table.

Claire turned on the water. "Why don't I wash up while you start looking at Jeffery's laptop?"

He nodded. "If it works."

She bit her lip. "Yeah."

She turned away then spun back. "I just realized...that guy knows you're helping me."

He shrugged. "Maybe. Or maybe he thinks I've been helping Jeffery."

****

After washing the dishes, she found Brad poring through files on Jeffery's laptop.

She joined him at the table. "Hey, you got into it."

He didn't glance up. "He hasn't changed his password in years. Fortunately, it booted up, but I haven't found anything useful yet." He plucked an envelope from his jacket pocket, which hung over the back of his chair. "Here, why don't you look this over? I found it taped under the pool table."

"How in the world did you think of looking there? You're a better detective than I thought."

He shrugged. "It was something Jeffery said once."

She removed four sheets of paper from the envelope. A computer printed spreadsheet spanned the pages with headings and columns of information. The first held dates followed by two cash columns, *Paid* and *Sold*. She scanned all the pages, cash amounts ranged from eight-hundred to ten-thousand dollars. A column headed *Product* followed. She scanned down, frowning at the three letter codes. The next were *Location 1* and *Location 2*. Then there was a final one for comments. If there were any, they were short and cryptic. What could *dt pu -15 term*, or *jk lst use* mean?

All the dates were in order and started about three years ago, ending a month earlier. That must have been when

Jeffery had printed the list. Not likely that this, whatever it was, had ended. She called up a calendar on her new phone. Every date was a Monday. Some were two in a row, but most were every other Monday. There were a few gaps of three weeks.

She bit her lip to the point of pain. She didn't want to ask, but had to. "Do you think this is Jeffery's? Do you think he was involved in something illegal?"

He took her hand. "No! He wouldn't do that, and besides, he told you he wanted your help figuring something out."

"But, he could've been trying to extricate himself from this." She waved the papers at him.

He faced her and took her other hand. "Claire, you know him better than that. He probably stumbled on something and wanted to solve it himself."

She nodded. He was right. Jeffery would never do anything illegal.

She sighed, stared at the pages. "Whatever this person is doing, it pays well. Do these phones have internet access? I think we should take pictures of these pages and upload them to my cloud account. We wouldn't want to lose them."

He grabbed his phone. "They do, but—" He checked the screen. "Looks good. Why don't you give it a try?"

With her new phone in hand, she flattened each page, snapped pictures and uploaded them.

She opened her notebook, wrote down all the codes under *Product* and recorded how many times each was used. There were five products. One was added near the end, listed three times in the last couple of weeks. Another was dropped halfway through the list.

She frowned at her new list. "I wonder what these people are buying and selling."

Brad glanced at her. "It could be drugs, guns, maybe

even escorting illegals across the border."

Claire showed her list to Brad. "There are five different items with codes of three letters. They've bought and sold the most of this." She pointed to the letters *LMG.*

"That's light machine gun."

Her mouth dropped open. "They're running guns? Lots of guns." She dropped her gaze to the long list.

"Apparently."

He didn't seem phased. "I'm about ready to search the first flash drive." He fished them both out of his pocket, and stuck one in a side slot on the laptop.

"Why don't I check the other?"

Brad slid the laptop over. "Here, you take this one. I'll get mine."

Claire spent the next half hour attempting to compare the files on the flash drive to files on the computer. It appeared the flash drive was a backup. She leaned against the back of her chair, frustrated. Did Jeffery hide files on the flash drive among the regular backup files? Not every folder on the laptop was copied to the flash drive. It was going to be tedious comparing folder by folder.

"Do you know a way to compare two drives?" She tapped the screen. "I think this is a partial backup of the laptop, but maybe there are extra files hidden on the flash drive."

He dragged Jeffery's computer toward him. "That's a good idea. There's a program that syncs the files on two devices and gives you two lists, each one showing what's missing from the other device." He typed for a few minutes.

"There." Brad turned it back toward her. "I hope it finds something."

"Thanks." She dropped her gaze to the computer, set up the search and the screen displayed file after file. This would take a while.

"Do you want some coffee?"

"Yeah, that'd be great."

Derrick had taught them how to make coffee with the old percolator when they were kids, years before he allowed them to have any. When they were young, Derrick was the only one to cook. He'd make bacon and eggs or pancakes and sausage for breakfast. The three of them took turns with breakfast chores. One would make Derrick's coffee, one would set the table and the third would wash up afterward.

Claire missed those days. When she was at the cabin with the guys, she could forget about her parents arguing and the tension at home. She'd challenged the guys, whether it was hiking, swimming or chopping wood. It was a peaceful world, separate from her normal one. And now a scary world had come to haunt the cabin.

She sighed then dumped the morning's coffee grounds in the trash. She prepared the pot, put it on a burner and turned the stove on, adjusted the flame, and got out fresh cups. As she set them on the counter, arms snaked around her from behind and she jumped.

"Sorry. Are you okay?"

"I found out I was tricked into divorcing Jeffery and now he's dead. I was almost killed and I'm wanted for his murder. Why wouldn't I be okay?" Her voice trembled.

He tightened his arms around her. "We'll clear this up."

"I sure hope so, but it won't bring Jeffery back." She leaned her head back against his chest. "It's not the same here anymore. I can't block out the rest of the world."

He kissed the top of her head. "You were different here when we were kids, happier, more daring than at home."

She nodded. "I felt safe here. I needed you, Jeffery, Uncle Derrick *and* this place." A tear slipped down her cheek. She brushed it away.

She dropped her hand onto the arms encircling her. He

made her feel safe and comforted. She hadn't been held in so many months. Brad still cared for her, and the loneliness and pain receded a little.

She realized she'd been hearing the perking of the water for a while. How long had Brad's arms enclosed her? The coffee color was almost perfect. A good, long while, then.

She didn't want him to let her go, but they couldn't stare at the pot any longer. "Coffee's ready."

He released her.

She gazed over her shoulder at his face and back down again. "Thanks. I needed that."

He put the edge of his finger under her chin and lifted her head until she gazed at him. "Anytime." He gave her a small smile and stretched past her, lifting the pot.

She side-stepped as he poured coffee into the cups.

****

Brad stared into his cup after he set the pot back on the stove. His empty arms ached for her. He hadn't imagined how good it would feel having them around Claire. He chastised himself. His best friend had been married to his second best friend. Jeffery was murdered yesterday. He pulled in a deep breath and returned to his seat beside Claire.

She stared at the computer screen. "There are two files on the flash drive that aren't on the computer. The first is the printout you found. Jeffery was probably making sure the file didn't get lost."

She double-clicked the second file. "I think these are Jeffery's notes. There's an explanation of some of the abbreviations on the spreadsheet. You were right about *LMG* and *HSA* is handgun semi-automatic." She pointed at the screen. "Dean Crowley's name is on here, which is probably why he killed Jeffery."

Brad scooted his chair closer, and read the notes. "So, Jeffery thought Crowley reported to somebody, but he didn't know who. I wonder if he'd figured it out and that's why he wanted to talk to you. Is this someone on the force or another scumbag gun runner?" He stood. "What's the date on this file?"

She clicked on the folder behind the open document. "About a month ago. Jeffery could have learned a lot in a month."

"Enough more to get himself killed."

She gasped.

He patted her shoulder. "Sorry. Why don't you save both these files to your account, too? Then we'll do the compare on the other flash drive."

She uploaded the files and switched drives, setting up the compare program. "It's past lunchtime. Why don't we eat while we wait for this?"

"Good idea." Brad stood and stretched. They worked together making ham sandwiches and grabbed sodas.

Claire stared out the window. Only a few fluffy clouds hung in the sky. "Do you think we'd be safe enough sitting on the back porch?"

Brad paused as he lifted his plate and gazed at the woods. The river sparkled here and there through the trees. "It should be fine." If someone got as far as the back porch, searching for Claire, they'd see the cars and know she was here anyway.

She juggled her plate and glass to get through the door. Brad followed her. They sat on each side of the round table, slanting their chairs to have a view of the backyard.

She took a deep breath and relaxed her shoulders. "It's been over a year since I've been here. I'd forgotten how peaceful it feels."

He tipped his chair back against the house wall and

closed his eyes. In the distance, the river rushed over rocks. Birds called from the trees. He opened his eyes as a chipmunk peeked out of the stacked wood. "I was here a couple of months ago. We hiked, caught fish for dinner and drank too much beer."

And talked about Claire. Sometimes Jeffery was inconsolable in his need to get her back. Even if she'd never taken Jeffery back, Brad wouldn't be able to have her himself. Jeffery still loved her too much and he wouldn't hurt his friend. With Jeffery gone, however, he'd be able to have a chance with her. A stabbing pain twisted his heart for even considering it less than twenty-four hours after his friend's death.

He bounded up, his chair crashing back to the floor.

Claire gasped and whipped around. "Brad?"

He fled down the steps. "I need a little time." He couldn't help the gruff way he sounded. He made a beeline for the river.

Chapter 4

Claire stared after Brad. He'd talked about spending time here at the cabin with Jeffery. She covered her lips with her fingers. It was grief. He had to be in so much pain, knowing he'd never be here again with Jeffery, or anywhere. They'd been closer than brothers. She blinked back tears. It hadn't been a full day since Jeffery's murder. Brad had been so busy helping her he hadn't had time to deal with his feelings.

Claire had grieved the end of her marriage many months ago. In the last couple months she'd healed enough for them to talk. She'd thought they might work toward mending their friendship. His death hurt her, especially the way it happened, but Brad lost his best friend and it probably was only now beginning to sink in. He had to be hurting so much.

She took a deep breath and stood, searching the edge of the woods and what little she could see of the river, but he was already out of sight. She picked up their dishes and headed back into the cabin. There was still a lot to do.

After she sat at the kitchen table, she pored through the files on Jeffery's laptop in case Brad had missed anything. She stretched her back and checked the time. Almost an hour and Brad hadn't come back. She couldn't put off opening the only unmatched folder on the second flash drive, *My Vacation*. Jeffery hadn't taken a vacation since they'd been divorced, and in the three years they were married, she'd only gotten him to take one. If this file had been their vacation, he would have called it *Our Vacation*.

The back door opened. She spun around, her heart pounding, afraid she'd find a gun pointed at her.

She held back a laugh when Brad stepped in, wet hair dripping into his face. She scanned down his body at his soaked clothes making puddles on the floor.

"Did you fall in? It seems a little early in the season for a swim."

He closed the door and spilled more water when he kicked off his shoes. "Not really."

Did that mean he jumped in on purpose?

When he lifted his arms to pull off the shirt, his abs rippled. He looked cold and hot at the same time. She itched to warm him with her body. Instead, she turned back to the computer and forced herself to take slow, even breaths. What was wrong with her? She hadn't responded to a guy like that since, when? Never? With Jeffery, her love had blossomed over time out of their deep friendship in their teens. Although she and Brad had always been friends, this was over the top lust. Wasn't it? Probably because she hadn't had sex in almost a year.

"I'm going to take a hot shower. I'll be out in a few minutes." He escaped into the bathroom and closed the door.

She eyed the bathroom door. He hadn't gotten dry clothes. Very soon he'd stride between the bathroom and bedroom with only a towel wrapped around himself. Short, shallow breaths claimed her. All thoughts centered on imaginary scenes of a lost towel.

She needed to do something. She couldn't sit here and allow herself to stare at him when he came out of the bathroom. Coffee. Brad was cold. Coffee would warm him up and give her something to do.

****

Brad closed the bathroom door and peeled off his clothes. He realized he should have grabbed dry clothes first. He stared down at the wet pile on the floor. He wasn't putting those back on. He'd have to wrap in a towel when he finished and not glance at Claire.

The hunger on her face had taken him by surprise. Then she'd turned away and he wondered if he'd imagined it because that's what he wanted to see. He didn't want to test his control if it happened again.

He'd always had a low simmering attraction to Claire. More than friendship, but the simmer was turning into a boil. To cool off his thoughts and libido he'd jumped into the river. He'd swum up the river and let it drift him back down several times before he'd regained control again. Then he'd almost lost it when nice warm Claire stared at him for a moment before turning back to the computer. She didn't have to touch him to warm his cold and shivering body.

Stepping under the warm spray, he reminded himself the woman on the other side of the door had been married to his best friend. They may have been divorced, but she'd just found out she'd been tricked into it. She might be thinking about all the things that could have been if the deception had never happened. She wouldn't be ready to start a new relationship and he wasn't ready to take that step with his best friend's ex-wife yet, either.

He recalled her face, and he stifled a moan. He couldn't have her knocking on the door, asking if there was a problem. He might be too weak and ask her to come in. If he stood naked before her, she would know exactly how he wanted her. He'd take his time advancing on her. Would she back out the door and close it in his face? If not, he'd make short work of getting her out of her clothes. The images vanished when he thought of the shower with barely enough space for him to turn. The floor wasn't much better.

He shook his head and turned the water to cool.

****

The bathroom door opened behind her and the bedroom door closed. Disaster averted. She poured two cups of coffee and carried them to the table.

A minute later, Brad returned to the table, picked up his cup, and took a sip. "Thanks. This is exactly what I need." He shifted the chair inches from hers and sat. "So, what did you find?"

She could do this, for Jeffery. "There was one unmatched document on the other drive titled *My Vacation* and you know he didn't take one. It's Jeffery's journal of the case. About a year and a half ago, he pulled over a speeder and ended up searching the trunk, finding a case of guns. He called for backup. The guy was arrested, and the car and guns impounded. The guy died in jail. It was ruled a suicide, but Jeffery didn't believe it. He drove behind the tow truck going back to the station, so there was no way for the guns to not get there. They disappeared before they got to evidence."

She stared at Brad. "He wasn't a detective. He should have turned it over to you."

He banged his cup down and coffee sloshed over the rim. "He never approached me with this. Did he think I was in on it?"

She put her hand on his arm. "He wouldn't. There's no way he'd think that of you." She squeezed his arm. "Don't you report to the sheriff?"

"Yeah, everyone knows I report to Crowley on internal affairs." It was a small office and fortunately, a rare duty. He ran a hand through his hair. "So, Jeffery must have known early on Crowley was involved in this and either figured I'd have to report to Crowley or didn't want to put me in the middle of it. But I would have taken it over Crowley's head to the Bureau of State Investigations."

Claire turned back to the computer. "That covers what I've read so far."

They shared the screen and read.

She gasped. "He found out!"

Brad caught her eye. "What? I didn't get that far."

She pointed to the screen. "Jeffery found that woman and she told him that Dean Crowley paid her to put something in his drink, call me and then pretend to have sex with him. He talked to her a couple months ago and he never told me."

She slumped back in her chair. "I wouldn't have let him tell me anyway." Maybe if he'd started it right, she would have let him finish.

"I'm glad."

She rounded on him. "What?"

He held up a hand. "*Not* that you wouldn't let him tell you, but that he talked to her. He knew, in his heart he hadn't cheated on you, but sometimes, when he was most depressed, he believed the evidence. So, I'm glad he found out the truth."

She nodded and blinked back tears, covered her mouth for a moment. "He always told me he couldn't remember being with her. I thought he was lying." She choked on the words.

He patted her arm. "Let's get back to this."

She wiped her eyes, took a couple deep breaths and a sip of her coffee. Jeffery hadn't tried to talk to her since he found out, so she couldn't berate herself for not listening.

They finished the document and Claire sat back in her chair. "Jeffery did pretty well for having no formal training in investigation."

He slammed his hand on the table. "It would have gone

faster if he'd come to me, without putting himself in danger."

She sighed. Maybe Jeffery would be alive and they'd still be married. "So, now what? There are still holes. Jeffery didn't find out who Crowley's working with."

"On Monday, I'm going to call State and talk to an agent. I'll send him all this." He waved at the table. "And we'll set up an investigation."

Brad checked his watch. "How about a hike and then we'll cook dinner?"

She bit her lip. "Is it safe?"

He shrugged. "Probably safer than in here."

Chapter 5

Brad enjoyed making the simple dinner of hamburgers and salad with Claire. It reminded him of the times he'd had dinner with her and Jeffery.

He sat at the head of the table and across the corner from Claire. He shifted and bumped her knee with his and shifted away. Her gaze flashed to him. Had she felt the same little jolt?

They needed a distraction. "I've seen your byline on a few major stories."

She nodded. "I've gotten more good assignments. I've had more time the past few months to work on them."

She probably had to fill in the time she would have spent with Jeffery. It must have been hard for her to leave him.

"I'm sorry I wasn't there for you after you left Jeffery. It hit him so hard, I couldn't do it."

She nodded, and turned her head away. "I understand. I'm glad you were there for him. It was so unfair." She blinked a few times.

"For both of you."

She closed her eyes and took a deep breath then beamed. "So, tell me about your house."

He let her change the subject.

"It's coming along." He'd sold his last house after doing major renovations on it and purchased the next one just before Claire left Jeffery. Although she'd been to the old house many times and watched his progress, she'd never been to the new one.

"I did the master bath similar to the old house." Claire had helped him pick out the fixtures and tile so it was easier to do the same. "The old cast iron sink was too heavy to lug down the stairs, and since it would fit through the window, I decided to toss it out. One of my hands slipped and the sink flipped and crashed into the deck."

She covered her mouth with one hand, but her eyes showed her merriment. He hadn't seen her smile since before she left Jeffery.

"I was going to replace the deck down the line, but it became my next project."

She laughed and he joined her. It was good to see.

They continued talking for a while after they'd finished their meal, and he glanced at his watch. "I'm going back to my place tonight. I need to check my home phone and turn on my cell." And probably sleep better not being in the room next to Claire's. Or maybe not because then he'd worry about her.

Claire's stricken face made him clench.

"I thought you were staying here tonight."

"I'm sorry. I have to show up at home. If Crowley can't contact me, he may guess I'm with you. I'll be back tomorrow morning." He ran the back of his fingers down her cheek. "Be careful. We don't know how long it'll take for someone to figure out Jeffery owned this cabin and look here for you."

She sighed. "All right. You be careful, too."

"Why don't you give me your apartment key? I'll see if I can get in and pick up some clothes for you."

"Didn't you say you couldn't go to my place?"

He shrugged. "Yeah, but I'll scope it out. If it's clear, I'll go in."

She retrieved her keys, slid off her house key, and held it out. "Can you get my laptop, too?"

"Sure." Their fingers brushed as he took it. He kissed her forehead, and wished he didn't feel like he was hurting her by leaving.

After an uneventful drive, Brad circled the block of Claire's apartment complex then entered the parking lot. He drove down the center of the lot and scanned for occupied cars. Of course, someone could have seen him drive in and ducked down. He parked near the third building of the six facing the lot and studied his surroundings for several minutes. No one reacted to his arrival, so he sauntered up to the door, used her key to let himself into the main hall and took the stairs to the second floor. Each building contained twelve apartments, four per floor. Claire's apartment was the back right corner.

He unlocked her door and wrapped his hand around the flashlight. He'd never been to Claire's apartment, but in the small space, it was easy to find her bedroom. A backpack sat on the floor of the closet. The zipper rasped open and he dropped in hiking shoes, and two pairs of jeans. He chuckled at the row of t-shirts hanging in the closet and took down four. At the dresser, he hesitated then tugged a drawer open. He grabbed a stack of panties and shoved them into the pack. In the drawer beside it, he found bras. His fingers, skimmed a lacy one and he swallowed hard as he pictured it barely covering Claire's breasts. He picked it up and two more plain ones. Last, he added a few pairs of socks.

In the bathroom, he opened the closet door. He found a small travel bag, opened it, finding all the necessities. He dropped it in the backpack. As he swung the door, he spied a box of tampons and added it to the pack.

He snatched up the laptop from the desk across from her bed, then yanked one strap of the backpack over his shoulder and headed out. At the apartment door, he listened, but didn't hear voices or footsteps, so he opened it far enough to peek into the empty hall. He locked up and headed to the exterior door. Halfway to his car, he passed a couple on their way in. He gave them a curt nod and kept going. Hopefully, they hadn't noticed him.

Back in his car, he took an indirect route home, and slid into his garage then grabbed his cell phone and battery from the glove compartment. He paused at the door to the house, withdrew his gun then yanked the door open and stepped inside. He swung the gun from one side to the other, and let out a breath.

The chair he'd shoved under the kitchen doorknob was still in place. A check in the living room found that chair in place as well.

Three messages waited on his answering machine. He hit the button. The first was a condolence message from one of the guys at the station.

After the beep, Crowley's gruff voice filled the room. "Hayes, where are you? Get yourself to the hospital ASAP." The message had been left at two-twelve that afternoon.

The third message was a hang up. Maybe it was Crowley trying again to contact him.

He turned his cell phone on and it chimed with messages.

The first was from Alex. Brad hadn't seen him in a couple of months, but they talked every few weeks. "Hi, Brad. I'm going to be visiting for Mom's birthday. Maybe we can plan something while I'm there. Give me a call."

Three weeks? Hopefully the case was resolved by then. He couldn't imagine Claire trying to hide out for that long.

The second call was Crowley. "It's Crowley. Hayes, I need to talk to you. Get to the hospital." The message was left at eleven-fifty.

The last call was from Tina, the day dispatcher at the station. They'd been on a couple of dates, but there'd been no connection with her. "Brad, I'm so sorry to hear about Jeffery. It was a horrible shock. Let me know if I can help." He could imagine how she'd want to help.

It was a little after nine o'clock. Since Crowley was sheriff, he'd likely be allowed visitors. Brad would rather have a tooth pulled than go see him.

****

Brad sauntered into the sheriff's hospital room. The top of the bed was in a sitting position, and the sheriff stared at a small TV screen on the wall.

"How are you doing, Dean?" He lowered himself into a chair next to the bed, dreading this talk.

Crowley glared and turned off the TV. "Dickens' bitch shot me. How do you think I'm doing? Hit my lung and then my scapula."

Brad suppressed a wince at Crowley's words.

The man was either cloyingly friendly or grouchy. This was the worst grouch ever, but he was probably in pain from the gunshot wound. A sling confined his right arm, and his normally ruddy complexion was pale. He probably worried, too, that he'd be found out.

Crowley deserved what he got and worse for murdering Jeffery and trying to kill Claire.

He had to be careful not to defend Claire or he'd give himself away.

"Where have you been?"

"I've been looking for Claire. I know a couple of places where she likes to disappear to. I even went to her apartment to see if she left anything to show where she'd gone."

"Why didn't you call her?"

"I tried, but she didn't pick up. I figured she was hiding from everybody."

"Never mind. I've got two of the others working on it. What I want you to do is find out what Jeffery Dickens was up to."

Brad frowned. "What do you mean, 'what he was up to'?"

"I was beginning to suspect he was involved in dealing guns."

Brad gripped his thighs, pushing his elbows out. "Jeffery? No way. He's the cleanest cop I know." Crowley must have been trying to get a reaction out of him. It would be unethical to ask this of him.

"You know how many cops start out clean and go bad?" Crowley asked. "Maybe the breakup with his woman screwed with his head."

Brad channeled his anger inside. He dropped his hands and balled up his fists. He eased out his breath, and masked his emotions. Crowley broke them up and it *had* screwed with Jeffery's head. He wasn't the same after Claire left.

"Yeah, he was messed up after that, but he still wouldn't have gone bad." He clamped his lips to prevent himself from saying more.

"Well, start looking into it for me anyway."

Brad stood. "All right. Anything else?" He needed to get away from Crowley before he did something to give himself away.

"That should keep you busy enough."

Brad frowned at him for a few seconds. "See you later, Sheriff."

He drove home on autopilot, half his mind going over Crowley's words. Why would Crowley tell him to investigate his best friend? Nobody should be put in that position. Was it only to keep him busy? Or to see if he'd protest? Maybe he should have. Or had Crowley fabricated evidence to implicate Jeffery in gun running since Jeffery couldn't defend himself? Jeffery wouldn't be involved, and the sheriff hoped there'd be no way to prove he wasn't.

Crowley was trying to cover his tracks.

Chapter 6

Brad did his regular Sunday morning run in case he was being watched. Everything was as always. An occasional dog barked, a man stepped out and picked up the morning paper from his porch, he nodded at a woman exercising her dog. After his run, he showered and headed to the *Captain's Net* for breakfast to listen for talk about Jeffery. He didn't go every Sunday, but often enough it wouldn't be suspicious.

Since there wasn't a hostess Sunday mornings, he seated himself in a booth beside one of the few windows. He chose the table next to the corner one, since that one was occupied by Bert and his wife. He'd still have a view of the entire room. It wasn't long before the perky blonde, Candy, brought him a cup of coffee.

She put her hand on his shoulder, leaned down close to his ear and whispered, "I need to talk to you." She straightened up and said, "The usual, Brad?"

He studied her. "Yeah, that sounds good."

She moved on to another customer.

Maybe she'd heard something.

He twisted in the booth, his back to the window. Most of the customers were Sunday regulars. It was still early, so less than half the tables were occupied.

Candy retrieved a pot of coffee and stepped from table to table, offering to top up cups. She seemed normal, not nervous. Maybe what she needed to talk about wouldn't put her in danger. She was enrolled at the police academy. Sometimes, if she had a break while he was eating, she'd sit down and ask him about his experiences. Occasionally, she'd join Jeffery and him. She was an enthusiastic student and couldn't wait until hands on training started.

Candy returned with his plate and refilled his cup. She leaned close and whispered in his ear. "When you're done eating, meet me outside the back door." He chuckled as if she'd told him a joke, but his stomach tightened. If she needed to talk in private, it probably was dangerous.

While he ate, he listened to conversations at nearby tables. There was talk of Jeffery's death in the parking lot, but no more than the buzz of an exciting event. They hadn't just lost their best friend of twenty years. He blocked the thought. It wouldn't help unravel the reason for Jeffery's murder.

Once he finished eating, he paid his bill and headed outside. He scanned the parking lot, turned right along the front and made his way to the back door, leaned against the building, and studied the parked employee cars.

After a couple of minutes, Candy stepped through the door, scanning the back lot as if worried she'd be seen. Her voice was barely above a whisper. "I was here Friday night."

His heart rate kicked up. He hoped she could clear Claire. "Did you see something?"

"I was taking a break, sitting on the bench out front, right beside the bush at the corner."

Brad listened as Candy described the same story Claire had told him. She couldn't tell what Jeffery and the Sheriff said, but she'd heard the muffled sound of a silencer.

Candy ran her fingers over her eyelids. She stared at him, her eyes glazed with unshed tears. "Brad, he shot Jeffery. I froze. I knew I'd be next if the sheriff noticed me. I stayed where I was until people poured out, then I mingled."

He squeezed her shoulder. "You couldn't have done anything to save him. The most important thing was you stayed alive." He scanned the area, still no one visible. "Have you told anyone else?"

She understood the danger she could be in, but she'd taken the risk to tell him.

She blinked a couple of times. "No. I didn't know who to tell. If the sheriff is bad, who else is?"

She'd seen Brad many times in the *Captain's Net* with Jeffery and sometimes Claire, too. It didn't hurt he'd sort of become her mentor. "Thanks for trusting me with this. You're right. I don't know who to trust either. I have to get some more information and go over Crowley's head. Go back inside. I think it's best if we get you out of town soon. Be careful." He squeezed her arm and released it.

A witness. Relief flooded through him like cold water on a hot day. He believed Claire, but they'd needed an unbiased witness against Crowley and Candy had answered their unspoken prayers. It gave him hope.

****

Brad took as much care getting to the cabin as he had Friday night, and parked beside Claire's car. She immediately answered his knock and he stepped in, studying her face. Her forehead wrinkled.

He wanted to touch her, but fisted his hand at his side. "Is everything okay?"

"It's fine. But, how am I going to help you when I'm trapped here?"

"We'll figure something out. Why don't we sit down and I'll tell you what's been happening?"

He followed her to the couch. She sat sideways with one knee drawn up, facing him.

He told her about his meeting at the hospital with Crowley, and she didn't hold in her outrage. "He'll try to pin this whole thing on Jeffery, who's not even here to defend himself."

"We'll have to be his defense. Now for the good news. I found a witness. Actually, she found me."

She frowned. "A witness to Jeffery's murder?"

"Yeah."

She grabbed his arm with both hands. "Someone saw Dean shoot Jeffery?" She squeezed his arm harder. "Does he know? Her life's in danger."

He patted her hand, and she released his arm like it had become too hot. The imprints from her fingers remained. "Sorry." She rubbed one hand back and forth over the marks, only stopping when he put his hand over hers.

Her touch sent warmth up his arm and into his chest, but he shut it down. His energy needed to be focused on saving Claire. Dropping his elbows to his knees, he let her hand slide off his arm and hoped she didn't realize he'd withdrawn from her touch. He clasped his hands together.

She blew out a breath. "Can't we have Dean arrested for murder and then work on his dealing guns?"

"We need more proof and a motive. I'll discuss it with the agent tomorrow. Right now, why don't we organize Jeffery's notes? We don't even know what we know."

Always one for diving in, she jumped up. "All right. Let's sit at the kitchen table." Once seated, she turned on Jeffery's laptop, opened the journal and loaded a blank document. She made columns labeled, *What We Know, What We Need to Know* and *How to Find Out.*

They discussed the case and she typed information into appropriate columns. She leaned back and rolled her head. "Anything else?"

"That should be good. Upload it to your account and copy everything onto a flash drive so I can take it with me."

She copied files and handed him the drive.

"Now, how about a hike in the woods?"

Claire stood and stretched. "I'd love to get out."

She slipped on her shoes and they headed out the back door. He followed a path they'd memorized as kids, now narrowed from disuse. He'd always been the leader, except when Uncle Derrick joined them. The rush of the river became louder the closer they got to it. Their path ended at the river path, and he turned left. Spring runoff caused the river to overflow its banks and run faster than usual. Brad didn't bother trying to talk since the roar of the water would drown him out.

As a kid, he used to sneak out early and climb the hill in hopes of catching the sunrise and then sneak back into bed before anyone else woke up. They'd teased him for being a sleepy head, and he let them. He'd needed time alone to start the day.

They arrived at the waterfall, and he kept going, scrambling over and around boulders in the path as he climbed. He made it to the top, as Claire came up the last few feet behind him, stopping at his side.

"It's been years since I've been here," she said between pants. "Jeffery always headed in the other direction."

"I like this climb." Brad grinned. "He always complained when I took him this way." Brad put his hands on his hips as he waited for Claire to catch her breath. "Just a little farther. I like the view from the top of the next hill."

She waved at the path. "I'm ready."

Brad led the way. The path was flat again, with a view between trees of the river. Before long, they climbed again. They reached the top, and he sat on the huge, smooth rock slab. He stretched his legs in front of him and leaned back on his arms, his hands warmed by the sun-drenched rock.

Claire dropped down beside him, mimicking his position. "I forgot about the great view."

A few cars traveled on the highway about a mile away. A smaller creek divided the land halfway between them and the road. It wouldn't be long before new leaves obscured the view of the stream.

What used to be a corn field on the edge of town, now included soccer and football fields, basketball and tennis courts and a half full dirt parking lot. A soccer game was in progress. One team's navy blue shirts mingled with a yellow-shirt team. To their right, taller buildings in town hid the residential area beyond them, although the tallest were only four stories high.

Claire closed her eyes and tipped her face up. "I love the spring sun. It's just the right amount of warmth. We should have packed a lunch."

Brad couldn't take his eyes off her. She leaned back with her face to the sun, as if allowing it to worship her. Her hair flowed down, almost touching the rock beneath her. The sunlight turned the brown strands almost golden. Then she turned her head and opened her eyes. His imagination told him her eyes begged him to kiss her, and he wondered what she see when she gazed at him.

He stared into the distance. It wasn't the right time. He drew his legs up and rested his arms on his knees. Claire wouldn't be able to see his face or anything else as he recovered. The last couple days reminded him of when he'd been in his teens with a yearning to kiss and touch her.

****

She found Brad watching her with the same hunger as when she'd come out of the shower. Hungry. For her. One of her teenage fantasies played in her head. The one where Brad eased closer and closer until their lips touched. He turned away before she could decide if she wanted to play out that fantasy.

Claire faced forward. A bird could have hovered a foot in front of her and she wouldn't have seen it. Her concentration centered on each breath, in and out, restoring control of her emotions. No reason to hyperventilate. She had to have misread Brad. There was no way he'd been about to kiss her. He'd probably turned away because she'd been married to his best friend, who'd died only two days ago.

She caught movement out of the corner of her eye.

He stared at her again. "He left you everything, you know."

She'd half heard what he said, too intent on his eyes and fantasies. "What?"

"After the divorce, Jeffery made a will leaving everything to you. While you were married, you would have gotten everything anyway, but he wanted to make sure you still did."

She blinked back tears. She'd treated him like the pariah her father was and he'd done nothing wrong. "I wish I could go back and change how I treated him. Maybe he would have confided in me sooner. Before…this happened."

His hand squeezed and released her shoulder. "You did nothing wrong. *He* didn't even know if it was true."

She gazed out over the trees. All she could do for him now was make sure Dean Crowley paid for murdering him.

Wills reminded her of funerals, and she gasped, sitting straight.

He whipped his head around to check out the direction she'd been staring. "What did you see?"

"I just realized I can't attend Jeffery's funeral."

He took her hand. "I'm sorry, Claire. We'll do something here for him."

She squeezed his hand. She couldn't ask for his forgiveness, couldn't say a last good-bye. She'd always feel she'd wronged him.

Without releasing her, he stood. "I think we should head back." He helped her up, and kissed her forehead before leading the way back to the cabin.

Chapter 7

Brad signed in and accepted a *Visitor* badge then followed an assistant to the agent he'd talked to earlier.

The man knocked on a door frame. "Here's your appointment, Matt."

The agent stood and held out his hand. "Matt Richards."

Brad took his in a firm handshake. "Brad Hayes."

Brad studied the agent as intently as he was being assessed. Would this man believe him? The agent's dark brows lowered over his squinting eyes, then gave an over-the-top friendly smile. Richards rubbed his close cropped hair.

They sat and Richards spoke first. "So, you need our help resolving corruption in your department?"

"Yes. I only became aware of it after one of our deputies was killed."

"Oh, yes. I heard about that. They're looking for his ex-wife in connection with his death and the sheriff's injury."

"She wouldn't kill Jeffery."

Richards' eyebrows rose. "A lot of people have killed their ex."

"Not Claire. Her version is Sheriff Crowley shot Jeffery Dickens and then was going to shoot her. She grabbed her ex-husband's gun and shot the sheriff."

"That doesn't sound plausible. You've seen her? You know where she is?"

"I only talked to her on the phone and no." The easiest way to show corruption was to question Jeffery's death, which meant he had to tell what Claire knew about it. It was a risk, but one he had to take.

Again, the agent's eyebrows rose.

Brad shifted in his chair. Richards didn't seem to believe him. If their positions were switched, he probably wouldn't either. Maybe a change in topic would help. "I have a witness who corroborates Mrs. Dickens' version of the event."

"I'd like to talk to your witness."

Brad shook his head. "Not yet. I'm going to keep my witness hidden for a while longer."

He removed the flash drive from his pocket. "It turns out Deputy Dickens had stumbled across a gun running scheme and been investigating the sheriff for over a year. He should have come to me with his suspicions, but didn't. Apparently, he didn't talk to anybody about it. I found this at his house." He set the drive down in the middle of the desk.

The agent picked it up. "What am I going to find on here?"

"Details of Crowley's involvement. I haven't figured out yet what all he's selling, but light machine guns and handguns top the list."

Richards jammed the drive into a slot on his computer and opened a file. "This is a list of *What we know* and *What we need to find out.* Who's 'we'?"

Brad said nothing. He'd assessed each word before speaking, trying to make sure it sounded like he was doing this investigation on his own. He didn't think Richards would believe that any longer, but he wasn't giving Claire away. "I assume it's the royal 'we'. It was Jeffery's list, but I added to it." He was sure Jeffery wouldn't have minded this lie to protect Claire.

The agent's eyebrows rose, but he didn't ask

"Claire didn't do it. She wants to find out as much as I

do why Crowley killed Jeffery. Why don't you look through those files?" Brad nodded toward the computer. "It's pretty much everything Jeffery gathered. The journal ends about a month ago, so he could have found more after that."

"All right." Richards leaned forward. The only sound was the occasional click of the mouse.

Brad settled back in his chair and crossed his ankle over his knee. He hoped his jumpy nerves didn't show, that he appeared calm. The agent read through everything. A click and Richards' gaze roamed the screen as each file was opened. The agent grabbed a pad of paper from a drawer and started writing on it.

After about twenty minutes, he squinted at Brad. "It does seem like Crowley is involved in gun running. There may be other people in the department involved, too. There's not enough here to make any arrests."

Brad shook his head. "Jeffery wasn't a detective. He didn't know how best to pursue his investigation. I'm sure that's why he wanted to meet with his ex-wife. She's an investigative reporter. When I saw Crowley at the hospital on Saturday, he asked me to check into Jeffery's activities. He said he'd begun to suspect Jeffery of dealing guns. I think Crowley is going to plant evidence leading right to Jeffery, especially since he can no longer defend himself."

"I'm leaning toward believing you and Jeffery's investigation. But we need to get a lot more evidence, find out who's controlling Crowley and if there are others in the department involved." He leaned back and stared at Brad.

Brad hoped he had a good poker face as he waited.

The agent's expression changed, as if he'd come to a decision. "I shouldn't tell you this, but we got a call Sunday from Sheriff Crowley. He wants us to start an investigation into both Jeffery Dickens and you."

"Me?" Brad sat up straighter in his chair. He could see

how Crowley would try to implicate Jeffery, but how was the sheriff going to drag him into it? He'd be worried if he wasn't so angry. "He thinks Jeffery told me something. Or the guy who broke into my house reported back to Crowley I had Jeffery's laptop."

"Did you report this guy who broke into your house?"

"No."

The agent frowned. "Why not?"

Brad sighed. Another thing he shouldn't have mentioned. "I didn't want to tell why he broke in."

"So you got this from the laptop?" Richards lifted the flash drive.

He tried not to show surprise when Richards dropped the questioning about the break in. "Actually, no. I could have left the laptop. It didn't have anything useful on it. I got that from two flash drives in Jeffery's desk drawer."

Brad leaned back again. "I'd like to arrest Crowley for Dickens' murder, but I think we need to get more evidence about the gun running. I'd also like to protect my witness, and since I don't know if anyone else in the department is involved in this, I don't want to arrange anything through the normal channels."

"We can do that for you," the agent said. "I'll come to town tomorrow. I'd like to play it like I'm working with the sheriff."

Brad nodded and hoped it was only pretending. Maybe Richards believed Crowley's story and was stringing him along.

Chapter 8

Brad knocked at the door of the cabin. "Claire, it's me." The bags of groceries cut into his hand. He wished he could spend more time here with Claire. His greatest worry was that he'd show up and she'd be gone, taken by the gun runners.

She answered with a kitchen towel in her hand. "Brad, I didn't expect to see you today. Oh, more food. Nice." She tossed the towel on the counter as she let him inside. He put away the refrigerated items, as she waited, arms crossed, tapping her toe. Then he left the rest on the counter and followed her.

Claire sat sideways on the couch, facing him. "Tell me what's happening."

"Not much progress." He ran a hand through his hair. "I talked to Matt Richards at the state bureau. He's coming tomorrow. Oh, and Crowley called yesterday to ask them to investigate Jeffery and me."

She straightened her spine. "No! Why would he do that? What could that possibly do?"

"I have a feeling he's fabricating something. I'm sure Richards will find what Crowley wants him to and it'll look bad for Jeffery or me."

She put her hand on his arm. "There's nothing to find." Her frown turned to a grin. "I've been doing some research. I searched for crime stories in the state involving large numbers of handguns or machine guns."

He nodded. "That's a great idea. Any luck?"

"Yes. There was another cache of semi-automatics found in a car stop in the next county. It happened about three months ago and this time the guns made it into evidence. Unfortunately, the driver died under mysterious circumstances."

"So, it didn't look like suicide this time?"

She shook her head. "He seems to have slipped and fallen in the holding cell. He suffered a concussion and never woke up. The police didn't release whether it was an accident or if he was attacked. There wasn't any additional information about the guns, so maybe you could talk to them."

He nodded. "I'll do that." Maybe they were getting somewhere. He was proud of the way Claire found a way to investigate.

"There also seems to be an increase in crimes committed with light machine guns. Two fatalities so far."

"Hmm. I haven't noticed an increase here. I wonder if Crowley is trying to keep sales out of his jurisdiction."

He took her hand. He didn't want to tell her about Jeffery's parents. She hadn't seen them since she left Jeffery. They'd asked him a number of times over the last few months how she was doing. Claire now regretted leaving their son, and the guilt ate at her. "I talked to Ann and Jack this morning."

Claire's eyes watered and she blinked. Her hand trembled before she squeezed his. "They don't believe I killed him, do they?"

He shook his head. "Jack's words were, 'Claire couldn't possibly have murdered Jeffery. It had to be an accident.' I explained to them how it actually happened and they believed me. I also asked them to not discuss it with anyone."

"Thank you." She wiped her cheek when tears escaped.

"They're having the service on Wednesday. I asked if they'd give me some of his ashes to scatter here at the cabin. They thought Jeffery would have liked that."

She fell back against the couch and lay her head against Brad's shoulder. "I was right there, and I still can't believe he's gone. It's like a bad dream."

He kissed the top of her head. He wished he could do more for her. She was already dealing with Jeffery's death, she shouldn't have to worry about getting arrested for killing him. "I know. I'm keeping busy with Crowley and the case and then thoughts of Jeffery sneak in and hit me all over again. It's hard. I was closer to him than my own brother."

She rubbed her thumb across his hand.

Her hand belonged in his. When this was over, he would try his hardest to convince her they should be together. He wished he could take her far away from the pain and danger, but it was impossible.

"Do you want to stay for dinner?"

He checked his watch. "I have to get back, put in some more time today."

She nodded. "All right." She showed him the articles she'd found and he read through them.

"Thanks. I'll try to get back in a couple days." He kissed her forehead. It wasn't enough. He wanted to drag her into his arms and give her a real kiss. Instead, he stepped away from temptation and left.

****

Claire wanted to hug him and never let go. Long dormant feelings for Brad rose to the surface, but he probably still thought of her as Jeffery's wife. She sighed as she wrapped her arms around herself and leaned against the doorframe. Maybe they'd been friends too long for there to be anything more.

Brad and Jeffery had always been her closest friends. She'd always loved them. Her friendship for Jeffery had changed and grown to a different kind of love when they started dating. It had come to a painful, searing end when she found him with that other woman. If he had lived, and she'd found out the truth, her guilt might have still ruined a relationship with him. Knowing Jeffery, he would have found a way for her to forgive herself.

She sighed and stared into the woods. The men searching for her could find her at any time. She wouldn't know if they were in the sheriff's pocket, or honest officers. She might die in a staged shootout or make it to the station alive to die in an 'accident'. She shivered and stepped back into the cabin, locking the door.

****

It was after five by the time Brad stepped into his office. He wasn't sure if he'd be successful reaching the officer in charge of the gun find in the next county, but he'd give it a shot. After being passed around to different officers a couple of times, he finally found the man he searched for.

"This is Jason Miller."

Brad explained who he was and that he'd seen the article about the weapons Jason found. He told Jason they'd had a cache of guns disappear before getting to evidence, and the driver had apparently committed suicide. "I'd like to find out if you've gotten any more information on the source of your guns."

"Nothing more than you know," Jason said. "All we've had are dead ends."

"We've had a recent murder where the gun was left behind and it didn't have a serial number. Do your guns have numbers?"

"It was weird," Jason said. "Some did, some didn't. They must have come from different sources."

"Can you check them for me?" Brad asked. "I'd like to find out what types had serial numbers and which didn't. Maybe we can trace some of them."

"All right. I'll check and get back to you."

Brad took care of phone messages and leafed through paperwork left in his basket. His phone rang. "Brad Hayes."

"It's Jason Miller."

"That was fast."

"It's fast when there aren't any guns to look at."

"Yours are missing, too?" It shouldn't be surprising. He was surprised the guns made it as far as evidence.

"Yep."

"Did someone check them out?"

"No, I checked. Nothing on the sign out sheet. It's an empty box sitting on the shelf, so no one would ever know."

"We must both have people involved in this." This might be a huge operation.

"I also checked records for when the guns were brought in. There should be a list of the number of guns, types, and serial numbers. That's gone, too."

Brad shook his head. "They're thorough. I'll check more around here, try to see at what point our guns disappeared. Thanks, Jason."

"No. Thank you. It could have been months before anyone discovered the missing guns. I'll have to talk to internal affairs about it tomorrow."

Brad leaned back in his chair, wondering if people from any other stations were involved.

Chapter 9

At the station the next day, Brad arrived to a changed atmosphere. The other officers stood in small groups talking, and every once in a while, someone glanced at him and quickly away. A shiver crept down his spine. Maybe Crowley was leaking his lies.

He sat in his office, checking email when his boss, Tom Harkins, stepped in and closed the door. Brad frowned at him. "What's going on, Tom?"

Tom sat in the chair across from him, leaned back and joined his hands across his stomach. "That's what I'm here to ask you."

Brad lifted an eyebrow. "I have no idea." He nodded his head toward the common area. "It's weird out there. What are they talking about?"

"They're speculating. There's an agent from the state bureau of investigations talking to the sheriff."

"He's out of the hospital already?" Brad was surprised. Either Crowley was a tough guy or the injury wasn't as bad as he made out. Or he was too worried about covering up to let a gunshot wound get in the way.

"He got out yesterday. He shouldn't be back yet."

"And what's everybody saying?"

"They're wondering who the guy is investigating. Some are speculating it's you."

"Why would they think that?"

"You and Claire Dickens are good friends."

"Your point?" he asked through thinned lips. He

pictured Claire and how Jeffery's death affected her. This was hard on her and he couldn't tell anyone.

"Claire killed her husband and maybe you helped her get away."

"Jeffery was my friend, too." He pointed through his door. "Those people should know me better than that." Maybe he hadn't hidden well enough how important she was. "So, maybe we should wait to see what this agent has to say instead of speculating. How long has he been with Crowley?"

"About twenty minutes."

"Let's talk later when we know more." Brad stilled when he realized Tom eyed his hands as he played with a pen, flipping it over and over. If that wasn't a nervous giveaway, he didn't know what was.

Tom gave him an assessing glare, nodded and left.

He tossed the pen on his desk. He wasn't good at dishonesty.

Most of the people out there knew him. They shouldn't believe he'd be involved in his best friend's death. No matter how much he cared for Claire, he wouldn't help her if he believed she'd killed Jeffery. She'd be sitting behind bars.

A short time later, Brad glanced up from his work at a knock on the doorframe. Agent Matt Richards stood in front of him.

"Come in. How are things going?"

Richards stepped in and closed the door. He shook Brad's hand then sat down in a chair across from him. "I was with Sheriff Crowley. He's been lining up all his evidence against you and Jeffery Dickens."

Brad tensed. Crowley would have to do a lot of twisting to make the evidence implicate him and Jeffery. "It can't be too solid since I didn't know anything about this until four days ago." He leaned forward and rested his arms on his desk. "Crowley's saying he's been investigating Jeffery and me? What's his explanation for waiting so long to bring this supposed investigation to you?"

"He says Jeffery Dickens' murder brought it to a head. He's speculating that maybe Dickens' ex found out about his gun running and was afraid of him. Maybe that's why she divorced him. Maybe it was self-defense in the parking lot."

Brad leaned back and crossed his arms. Maybe Crowley was trying to force Brad to make a deal with the devil. Get Claire out of a murder charge and allow Jeffery to take the rap for the guns. "That's convenient. Did he give you any information you didn't already learn from Jeffery's investigation?"

"He said he saw you on three occasions transferring guns from your trunk to an unknown man's trunk."

Brad tamped down his anger. So, Brad had to go down, too, to save Claire. "He doesn't have pictures. I own a truck with no cap. That doesn't seem like a good way to transport contraband. Did he have dates and times for these events? If he'd seen me do it, he could have arrested me on the spot. It's his word against mine." Did Crowley think throwing this to the agent would remove him from suspicion? At most, it would delay the truth coming out. He hoped.

"He's being vague," answered Richards. "He wanted to gather more information before making an arrest."

"So, he has no evidence, only accusations. He called you to preempt my call."

"Pretty much."

"What's the game plan?" Brad gripped the arms of his chair.

"For now, you'll stay on the sidelines while my team starts the investigation."

"What? I brought it to your attention. I want justice for my friend. I want in on this." He didn't raise his voice. If he got too loud, others would hear.

Richards held up a hand. "You know you can't because you've been implicated. If during the preliminary investigation, you're totally cleared, I'll consider letting you join us."

Brad stood. "You have doubts about me." He supposed that was fair.

The agent propelled himself from his chair. "I have doubts about everybody. I need to get started with my own team. They're already talking to the other officers. I'd like to talk to your witness and get him or her into protection."

"You already know what my witness saw. Go on that assumption for now and I'll think about introducing you." Agent Richards was playing both sides in order to gather information, so Brad had doubts, too.

Agent Richards glared. "Have it your way. I hope your decision doesn't get your witness killed. I'll talk to you later." He stalked from the office.

Brad dropped into his chair. It didn't feel right not being a part of this investigation. He knew the locals better than an outsider. He needed to see this through. He needed to be the one to bring Crowley and whoever he was working with down. For Jeffery and Claire.

He headed to Tom's office, but found his door closed. Two muffled male voices drifted through the door, and he wondered if Matt Richards was talking to Tom. He slipped his hands into his pockets while he decided what to do next. His fingers closed around strange keys and he slid them out. He still had Jeffery's keys. He slipped them back into his pocket. He'd search the shed after dusk.

On his way back to his office, the buzz amongst the officers seemed louder. He approached a drinking buddy. "Dave, what's going on?"

Dave shook his head. "We just heard a police officer

was gunned down in his garage."

A charge jolted Brad. "Who? Where?"

Dave turned. "Hey, Zack. What was that cop's name?"

Zack frowned. "Jason Miller."

Brad's heart iced over and radiated through his torso and to his fingertips and toes. He'd gotten Jason killed. He choked the words out. "What do they know?"

Dave shrugged. "It was execution style. They don't have anything else yet."

Brad ran a hand though his hair. "Thanks."

He returned to his office, but couldn't work, and couldn't stop thinking about Jason Miller. How did someone find out within hours that Jason discovered the missing guns? He wished he hadn't called him. It hadn't gained him anything, but had cost a life.

These guys seemed to be one step ahead of them. The risk to Claire's life seemed to grow. He needed to keep her safe long enough to prove she didn't kill Jeffery.

****

After a tasteless dinner, Brad drove to Jeffery's neighborhood. He was more on edge than the last time he'd done this. Maybe Matt Richards had someone following him. He didn't see anyone, but might miss an expert investigator. He parked three streets from Jeffery's house and strolled, scrutinizing everything and everyone. Streetlights flickered on as he turned the last corner. When he was on the street behind Jeffery's house, he slipped through a side yard and bulldozed through the bushes into Jeffery's backyard. He slinked along the back, and stopped behind the shed. He hugged the side of the building until he stood at the front corner, and waited, listening for anything out of place. He crept up to the door, unlocked the padlock, and slipped it into his pocket. He didn't want anyone locking him into the shed. Stepping inside, he closed the door.

Without windows in the shed, he didn't worry about his flashlight being seen. He'd helped Jeffery take down tree limbs a couple of times, so he was familiar with the layout. Shelves lined the left, floor to rafters. The right side had one high shelf with equipment on the floor below. He started with the left.

Brad ran his light over every item on the top two shelves, moving bigger items to see behind them, opening cans and jars of screws. The third shelf held power tools. Paint cans filled the bottom shelf. He hauled them out two at a time and checked behind them. They were all oil based paints and stains, except one.

A small water based paint can was lighter than the others. He shook it. No paint sloshed inside. He picked up a paint can opener that sat on one of the other cans and opened the small can. A rolled up rag sat in the bottom. He shook it out and unwound it. Another flash drive sat on his palm. Brad was surprised at how ingeniously Jeffery had hidden some of his evidence. He must have known the danger he was in. It still hurt that he hadn't come to Brad. He slipped the drive into his pocket.

It was probably the only thing Jeffery hid in the shed, but he searched the rest of the space anyway, finding nothing more.

He turned off his flashlight, cracked the door open and peeked out. When nothing moved, he slipped out the door and replaced the padlock. He scanned the house, a flashlight flared across a back window. His heart slammed in his chest and he stepped behind the shed. He leaned his head against the wall. If whoever that was had heard him in the shed, they would have checked it first. He'd come too close to discovery. He willed his heart to slow, taking even breaths.

After about ten minutes, the back door creaked open, and Brad peeked around the corner of the shed. Footsteps clunked down the back steps, hitting the squeaky one. It might be Matt Richards' profile, but he couldn't be certain in the poor light. Brad ducked back and waited, kept his breathing even as his heart pounded. Would Richards head to the shed? There was no legal reason Richards would search the house at night. Proper protocol would be daylight with a search warrant and going in with a team. Bushes rustled on the far side of the yard and he let out a long breath.

Brad waited ten more tense minutes and worked his way back to his car the same way he'd come. He drove with care out of the neighborhood and headed for the highway. With little traffic, he was fairly sure no one followed, but took his normal precautions. He arrived at the cabin a little before nine and parked in back.

He knocked on the door and waited several minutes. "Claire, it's me." She wasn't expecting him and might have gone to bed, or thought he was the authorities. She let him in then closed and locked it behind him.

He hugged and released her, but she clung. He grasped her shoulders and nudged her back. "Claire, is everything okay?"

She nodded. "I hadn't heard from you so I was worried."

"I'm sorry. I got busy and forgot to call." He sat at the kitchen table.

Claire sat down across from him. "Um, did you talk to the policeman in the other department?"

"Yeah, and now he's dead." How could he protect Claire if a police officer couldn't protect himself against these people? He was screwing up as much as Jeffery had.

She covered her mouth, her eyes wide. "It's not your fault, Brad. You couldn't have known this would happen."

"He'd still be alive if I hadn't called him last night. He

checked evidence and found the box was there, but the guns were missing."

Claire squeezed his hand.

He pulled in a deep breath. "Jason may have talked to the wrong person or someone was monitoring the evidence. I'll have to see what I can find out." He ran a hand through his hair.

She gripped his arm. "Brad, be careful. You're in danger."

"No more than you are." They could both die trying to solve this.

He pulled the flash drive from his pocket. "I found this in Jeffery's shed. When I finished, someone was in the house. That was a tough twenty minutes."

Claire's hand quivered over his. "You could have been discovered."

He turned his hand over to hold hers. "I'm pretty sure it was Matt Richards, the state agent."

"So, he's started his investigation."

He shook his head. "I don't think so. He would have gone in there in broad daylight with a warrant and a team. Why go alone unless he didn't want the team to find something? Or he was planting something. Fortunately, I didn't tell him who my witness is when we talked earlier."

She frowned. "He's in it with Crowley?"

He shrugged and held up the flash drive. "Let's find out what Jeffery's put on here. Hopefully, it's not a copy of the other drives."

Claire retrieved the laptop from the coffee table and booted it up.

Brad plugged in the drive. "Two-hundred-forty-eight pictures."

He opened a program to view them and the first picture displayed. "I hope they're not all as dark as this one. I can't even tell what it is."

He skipped to the next. "I think this is the trunk of the car Jeffery stopped. He must have inspected the guns." He pointed to the bottom of the picture. "You can see the plate number."

They studied a few more pictures before Brad commented again. "There's Crowley." He stood at the back doors of a windowless van. The man beside him had his back to the camera. "I don't know where this is. The shot's too tight to see the surrounding area."

The next few pictures showed the doors open with boxes inside the van, some similar in size to the box in the car trunk. Both men carried boxes to the trunk of a car. Brad skipped ahead, stopped and swore at a close-up of the other man.

"Do you know him?"

"He's Agent Richards. I gave him the flash drive with everything we know about Crowley and the guns."

"So, at Jeffery's house tonight, he was making sure nobody would find anything incriminating when they do the official search." She gasped and clenched his arm. "Or he planted evidence. Brad, we're in so much trouble."

The fear in her eyes twisted his gut.

He wished he could take her in his arms and keep her safe. "I wonder why they haven't tried to kill me yet. They killed Jeffery, those two gun runners, and Jason Miller. As far as they know, I know as much as Jeffery and a lot more than Jason." A little knowledge was definitely more dangerous than a lot.

"Maybe they want you to lead them to your witness and me before they kill you."

"We're getting out of here tomorrow. All three of us." It got worse and worse. He couldn't trust anyone at his station. Now he couldn't trust anyone at the state bureau.

She touched his arm. "Let's finish going through the pictures. There may be more surprises."

Five cars were filled with boxes and each time the driver remained in the car and was handed a paper. The drivers and license plates weren't visible in any except the first one.

Claire tapped the paper being handed to another driver. "Do you think that's the address they're supposed to take the guns to?"

"Probably. It may tell them what route to take and what time to arrive. Maybe it tells them how they're getting paid, but the guns are probably already paid for."

Richards stood beside the open van door and Crowley's back was to the camera as he walked away.

"I think Richards was the one who acquired the guns. Why does he need Crowley?" Brad asked.

"Maybe Crowley determines where they go."

"I can see why Jeffery wanted to talk this over with you." At Claire's pained expression, Brad said, "I'm sorry. I shouldn't have said that."

She touched his arm. "It's all right. With as much as I've been going over all this, you'd think it would always be in my mind, but I try to block that part out." She laced and unlaced her fingers on the table, staring at them. "I wish I could go to Jeffery's service tomorrow."

Brad stilled them with his hand. "He'd understand. He'd want you to stay safe."

Brad wondered if the hurt in her eyes was because a friend died or if it was because the man she still loved died. Finding out in such a brutal way Jeffery hadn't cheated on her had to be traumatic, and maybe cause her so much guilt she wouldn't be able to let go of it.

He tore his hand away. "Let's get back to these pictures or I'll never make it home." He turned back to the computer and started advancing through the images.

The next pictures, dated two weeks later, showed two men transferring boxes from a car trunk to a garage. She pointed. "I think that car was used the previous week. Is it another load or has he been holding them for a week?"

"Jeffery must have followed it after watching more guns get loaded."

"Do you recognize the area?"

The car was backed into a driveway in front of a two car garage with one door open. It was too dark inside to see beyond a few feet. The next picture showed a box being carried into the darkness, followed by the closed garage door and the men shaking hands.

The following displayed the street signs, angled to show the names of both streets. "Walnut Street and Wild Meadow Lane. I'll do a drive-by to see if I can find it."

She gripped his arm, fear back in her eyes. "Maybe you shouldn't. I don't want anything to happen to you."

He covered her hand and squeezed. "I'm going to do a slow drive-by. No stopping. Hopefully, I can figure out which house it is so I can get an address."

Turning back to the computer, he scanned through the last few pictures. "Well, not the caliber of a detective, but Jeffery did give us more information with his photos." He glanced at her. "Can you upload these to your account?"

"Sure." She slid the computer in front of her and worked on it, glancing up when Brad stood.

He dropped his hand to her shoulder. "I'll pick you up mid-afternoon. I'm going to talk to my witness, go to Jeffery's service and then pick her up." He didn't want to leave her in the dark about the witness, but Candy was safest if nobody else knew.

"All right." She followed him to the door.

He paused with his hand on the doorknob, then gathered her into his arms. After a couple seconds, she circled his neck and laid her head on his chest. The timing sucked, but this felt right.

"Claire?"

When she tipped her head up, he kissed her. No forehead this time. Her lips were soft and responsive. He wouldn't push for more, but it was hard to let her go. He loosened his arms and put his forehead against hers. "I'll see you tomorrow."

She nodded and he stepped out the door, pausing until the deadbolt clicked.

They were getting deeper into this Crowley mess and he was afraid he wouldn't be able to get her out of it. A noose tightened around his neck with speculation of what Crowley and Matt Richards were cooking up. Time was ticking away to get it straightened out before they arrested him. And if he didn't, what would happen to Claire?

Chapter 10

Brad barely registered the minister's monotonous speech. Jeffery's parents sat beside him in the front pew. He studied Ann's profile. Her only child's death had devastated her. She must have sensed his gaze because she took his hand. He squeezed it. Brad saw through Jack's blank face to the pain that consumed him. His son meant everything to him. He would have trouble going on. And Claire. How was she handling this, alone at the cabin? At least here, they had each other.

The minister's voice grew louder and Brad focused on it.

"Now we have friends and family who would like to say a few words about Jeffery. We'll begin with Bradley Hayes." As the minister sat, Brad climbed the three steps to the podium.

He surveyed the crowd. Friends, family and officers had come to say farewell to Jeffery, including his killer. Claire deserved to be here, but instead, Crowley was. He hoped he'd make it through this.

Brad cleared his throat. "I've known Jeffery since we were five years old. He's been my best friend from the day his family moved in two doors down from mine. It's going to be hard to get used to not being able to call him up to invite him to have a beer, or watch a game or go fishing. His passing leaves a hole in my life as well as the lives of the many people he cared for." His voice cracked and he paused to regain his composure. "I hope you don't mind if I take a few minutes to tell you about the Jeffery I knew."

He stared into the crowd without seeing them. "We must have been about seven, when we played our first practical joke. The girl who lived on the other side of Jeffery," he wouldn't say Claire's name, "had gotten a bicycle. Jeffery took it from her yard and talked me into helping him put it high into a tree. When she found it missing, she cried. We felt so bad, we had to help her find it. We convinced her she was the one who spotted it in the tree, then Jeffery and I climbed up and got it down for her."

The audience chuckled.

He'd never played a joke on her again, at least not a mean one. He couldn't stand to be the cause of her tears.

He told other stories about how they broke their parents' rules so they could try new experiences.

"We were competitive in high school sports. In one basketball game, we'd made a bet on who could get the most baskets. We stole the ball, even from teammates, to get the chance to make baskets. We won the game and I won the bet by one basket, but we sat out the next game after the coach talked to us about sportsmanship."

Brad paused. A warmth filled his chest, as if Jeffery was right there with him. "In our junior year, a girl in our class got sick and needed several blood transfusions. Jeffery arranged to have Red Cross come into the school for donations and he promoted it. He made announcements on the PA system at school during homeroom and posted signs in the cafeteria. So many students participated, our local Red Cross didn't have a shortage that summer. The girl recovered and was back in school in a few months."

His gaze met the woman's, who'd been that girl, and she smiled at him.

"Throughout high school, Jeffery had been undecided about what he wanted to do with his life. He knew he wanted to help people. Near the end of our senior year, he heard shots up the road." Brad pointed to the door. "He hid and witnessed a police officer rescue a woman from a man with a gun. At that point, he decided that's what he wanted to do." Brad smiled. "I already had my course set, but Jeffery could be persuasive, so I joined the academy with him." He told stories of their early days as officers.

"I hope I've given you a picture of the Jeffery I knew." He turned his gaze toward the ceiling. "I'll miss you, my friend."

He blinked back tears as he shuffled back to his seat. The minister announced the next speaker and Brad clenched his hands as Sheriff Crowley passed the pew.

Ann took Brad's hand. She whispered her thanks and gave him a watery smile. He leaned in and kissed her temple.

Brad wanted to tune out Crowley's speech, but needed to hear what he said. He was surprised when the sheriff talked about how Jeffery gave of himself beyond his normal duties to help the community. He gave instances where Jeffery had given his time in the schools or special events. Most Brad already knew about.

The cynical part of him understood Crowley praised Jeffery to cover himself, but Brad appreciated him sharing stories of his selfless friend that others might not be aware of.

He ended with, "I regret the delay that prevented me from arriving in time to save Jeffery's life."

Brad's hand jerked, squeezing Ann's hand tighter and then he released it. He whispered in her ear. "Sorry."

He couldn't take her pained expression, so turned away. Obviously, Crowley wanted to make sure no one would think he was at fault, but it still was hurtful to Jeffery's family. He took slow even breaths to tamp down his anger. He couldn't show it or the sheriff might suspect he knew the truth. He kept his eyes downcast as Crowley passed.

Three more speakers followed and then it was over.

They stood and Ann hugged him. "Are you coming back to the house?"

He checked his watch. "Of course I'll come." This day was harder for her than him. He'd stay as long as he could.

****

With thoughts of Jeffery's service, memories flooded Claire. Everywhere she turned, another memory assailed her. When Jeffery was ten, Uncle Derrick stood beside him at the stove, showing him how to cook eggs. When they were twelve, they sat at the kitchen table as Derrick walked them through tying feathers to hooks before he took them fishing. Jeffery had the clumsiest fingers, but he wouldn't give up. Evenings at the cabin were spent playing cards at the table or the three of them lined up on the couch, reading. At bedtime, they climbed into their bunks, but didn't always go right to sleep. Sometimes they talked for hours. Those were special times for Claire. The lights were out and she could say things she wouldn't normally be able to tell Jeffery and Brad. Like when she'd discovered her parents had gotten married because her mom was pregnant, and when she found out her dad was cheating on her mom. They couldn't see her tears in the dark.

She wiped the wet trails off her cheeks. Too many memories surrounded her in the cabin. She threw together a sandwich, grabbed an apple, a bottle of water and her purse, and flung open the door. She'd go to the rock point where Brad had taken her.

This time the hike was no fun, merely a way to run from her memories. She sank down at the top, catching her breath. She held the cool bottle of water to her forehead for a few moments before twisting it open and taking a long drink. One corner of her sandwich was squashed, but still tasted good.

Her thoughts returned to Jeffery. Sheriff Crowley would have been at the service, while she had to hide out. How many people believed she had killed Jeffery while his killer pretended to be Jeffery's friend? She hoped the truth would come out and Crowley would pay. She wished she could march into the service and tell everyone what really happened.

Claire gazed out at the spring green trees and the glittering river, then tipped her head up toward the sky, closing her eyes. "Jeffery, I'm so sorry I didn't believe you about that woman. We lost all that time when I was so angry at you and you still protected me with your life. I hope you can forgive me."

Claire lay back, letting the sun above, and warm rock beneath her, chase away the chill. Tears squeezed through her closed lids and rolled down the sides of her face into her hair. Her mind wandered to another memory of Jeffery.

He laughed. "Claire, how did you do that?"

She stared down the front of herself at the jam dripping from her chest to the floor. "I didn't realize I had butter on my hand and when I picked up the jar, it slipped. I caught it, but it was upside down and all the jam spilled out. At least I didn't break the jar." She glared at him. "And stop laughing at me."

He laughed harder. She set the jar down and stalked him. He retreated, but she caught and hugged him. He tipped her head up and kissed her.

His laughter was gone and his voice husky. "Let's go shower."

"But—"

He kissed her again and led her to the bathroom. Once the water was right, he picked her up and stepped in, fully clothed. He turned her, rinsed the jam away and removed her clothes, then did the same with his own.

After they'd made love, he had to rush to work without breakfast, but said it was worth it.

She smiled. Remembering was bittersweet, but not painful, now that she knew Jeffery hadn't cheated on her.

The screech of a hawk jolted her to awareness. She stretched and scanned the area. A hiker could have come across her while she'd been lost in memories. She was sure everyone knew her face by now. A trail of dust billowed up the drive to the cabin. Brad had come early.

A dark, official car drove out of the trees. She ducked down and flipped to her stomach. Her heart pounded in her ears, and her breathing shallowed into pants. Two men she didn't know got out of the car. She backed away from the crest so only the top of her head and eyes peeked over the top. She couldn't tell if they were police or bad guys. Either was bad for her.

She gasped. She would have been in the cabin when those men arrived, except for the memories that had driven her out. Almost as if Jeffery had found a way to protect her. She blinked back tears.

She fumbled for her cell phone in her purse, and called Brad.

"Hayes here."

"Brad, it's me," she whispered.

"I'm headed outside. Hold on." There were muffled voices, a door closing, and then silence.

Finally, he spoke again. "What's wrong?"

She kept her voice low. "Two men just drove up to the cabin."

"Damn. Where are you?"

"On your rock. I was having lunch."

"Thank God. Meet me at the Delaney place."

It seemed like the perfect place to meet up. The cabin's

driveway exited onto a different road, so Brad wouldn't have to go to Jeffery's cabin. "Okay, I can get there."

"Good. When I pull up to their cabin, I'll call your cell. Stay on the back porch and don't come around to the front until you hear from me."

"They're going to get the laptop." Whoever was down there would find the information Jeffery had collected. If they didn't already know from Agent Richards.

"You're more important than the laptop. Stay hidden. My witness had to work until one-thirty, so I'm picking her up at home about two o'clock. I'm still going to be awhile."

"That's all right. Be careful." After she stowed her phone, Claire gathered up her lunch remnants and started her two mile hike to the Delaney place, in the opposite direction from the cabin. The turnoff for the Delaney cabin had always been a rarely used trail, so she was relieved when she found it. She took long steps, in hopes if those men took the main path, they wouldn't see this one had been disturbed.

Since it was mid-week, the Delaney's wouldn't be there. She hoped.

At the edge of the yard, she surveyed the house. If the Delaney's were there, the back door would be open, but it wasn't. She let out a breath and approached the cabin, taking the two steps with caution. She settled into a plastic chair at the side of the porch and stared into the woods.

The door was unlocked at Jeffery's cabin. She'd been in such a rush she hadn't locked it. When she didn't answer the door, they'd file in and guess she was nearby. Otherwise, why leave a door unlocked? And her car was there. They'd start searching the trails. Maybe they'd call for backup. Unless they were the bad guys.

She caught herself tapping her foot and stopped. It wasn't loud, but she didn't know how far the sound would carry. She stiffened at a voice on the main trail and a squawk of the radio. Maybe they'd split up to cover both directions of the trail.

She was glad the porch was low enough there weren't railings when she dove off. She hit the ground and rolled under the porch, then wiggled closer to the house in hopes of hiding in the shadows. She curled up and forced slow, even breaths so she couldn't be heard, then hoped her pounding heart wasn't as loud as it sounded in her ears.

Her phone. Brad was supposed to call. What if he arrived while that guy was in the yard? She set it to vibrate, afraid to return it to her pocket. If they found her, she could dial Brad and he'd at least hear what was happening.

Her heart slowed until the first foot drop on a step. She closed her eyes then popped them open again. She wasn't a child who thought she couldn't see them so they wouldn't see her.

Footsteps crossed the porch and knuckles rapped on the back door. A few seconds later, the knock echoed again. Footsteps roamed above her and stopped. She stared at the boards. Her gaze darted to the edge of the porch and then above. He was probably peeking in the window.

A foot slid on the wood, then stepped down the stairs. His voice on the radio faded as he trekked farther away. "Nothing so far."

Her heart started to ease then her phone vibrated. How far did the sound carry? She hoped it was Brad, but also wished he'd been five minutes later. She couldn't hear the truck from under the porch, but maybe the man was close enough he could. She squirmed to the edge of the porch and peeked out.

Chapter 11

Brad headed back into the house, finding Jack first and told him he had to leave.

Jack gave him a bear hug. "Brad, it was so good to see you. And thank you for speaking. I didn't know some of those stories. It was good to hear them."

"I'll see you soon."

Before he found Ann, he stumbled across his father. He glanced around to make sure he wouldn't be overheard. He spoke in a low voice. "Dad, I'm going out of town for a few days. I'll talk to you when I get back."

Sam frowned. "Where you going, son?"

"I can't say and please don't tell anyone I'm gone."

Sam's eyebrows drew down. "I guess you know what you're doing."

"I hope so." He gave his dad a quick hug. Crowley would probably question his dad, but by that time, he'd already know Brad was gone. He would probably try to convince his father Brad was doing something illegal.

Brad found Ann taking more food out of the refrigerator and told her he needed to leave. She gave him a firm hug. "You take care of yourself." She hugged him again and whispered, "I don't want anything to happen to you, either."

"I'll be careful." He stepped back. Smart woman. She suspected he was headed into trouble.

He wished he could pick Claire up first, but he couldn't return to town with her to get Candy. He worked his way across town to Candy's house, keeping watch for a tail. He slid into a space beside her car, strode to the back of the large house and knocked on her door. She opened it immediately.

"I saw you drive up. Let me grab my bag." She turned back to her bedroom.

He stood by the door and took her bag when she returned. "Call your boss and tell him you had an emergency and you'll be out for a while. No sense making people think you've been kidnapped."

She made the call and turned off her phone, leaving it on the kitchen table.

He opened the door and peeked out to make sure it was clear before stepping through the doorway. At the corner, Brad waited for another tenant to enter a unit. They hurried to the truck and he helped Candy into the back, handing her the bag.

Once seated, he glanced in behind him. Candy had fastened the middle belt and lay on her side with her hand propping up her head.

He nodded. "That'll do."

He headed for the highway. "Have you figured out where you can stay?" He'd told her earlier it would be best if she stayed with a friend nobody in town would know about, rather than with family.

"Yeah, I wrote down a couple of phone numbers of people I can ask."

"We'll get you another phone when we're out of the area."

Her eyebrows pinched together. "This is for real, and we're all in danger, aren't we?"

He nodded. "I wish you weren't at risk, but I'm glad you witnessed the shooting, for Claire's sake."

Candy slammed her fist into her palm. "I want to make sure he pays for killing Jeffery."

They passed the town limits, he checked the mirror

again. The last car had turned off about a mile ago. "You can sit up now."

Candy sat up and tightened her seatbelt. She glanced out one side window and then the other. "So, why did the sheriff kill his deputy?"

"You sure you want to know?"

"I can't be in any more danger than I am already."

"Jeffery suspected Crowley was running guns and started investigating him. Crowley found out. We don't know how."

"For real?"

Brad let out a breath. "For real."

She grinned. "I feel like I'm in a movie."

He glanced at her through the mirror and shook his head. "Candy, at the end of the day, actors go home, safe and sound. Just remember, this is real, and if we're not careful, we could die like Jeffery."

Her smile disappeared. "I know, Brad."

Instead of doing his normal turn around after passing the side road, Brad turned on the road to the Delaney place, one road before Jeffery's. Keeping watch behind him, he turned right into the driveway and drove up to the house. He called Claire on his cell phone. It rang until it dropped to voicemail.

"Claire, where are you?" he whispered. He dialed again as he watched the right side of the house, afraid he was too late. Or maybe she'd fallen or was stuck somewhere along the trail. He blinked as a flash of color ran in front of his truck from the left.

Claire jumped into the seat and buckled. "Go now! Hurry!"

He put the truck in gear and backed around, throwing dirt up. "Claire, what's wrong?"

"Later. Just go." Hair was plastered to her forehead and she raked it back then dropped her head against the headrest, closing her eyes. She took deep breaths.

He dropped it into drive and the truck jumped forward. At the road, he turned right to take back roads. He didn't want to chance running into anyone searching for Claire on the main road.

"Hi, Claire," Candy said from the back.

"Candy. So, you're Brad's witness."

"He didn't tell you?"

She shook her head. "Brad was probably afraid I'd be captured, and tell them about you."

He couldn't tell her she was right, so he sent her what he hoped was an apologetic look. If she'd been captured, Candy would have been her only means to get free. He was still afraid she wouldn't survive long enough for Crowley to be arrested for murder. It wasn't his job to hide witnesses, but he didn't trust anyone else to help.

When they stopped at the end of the road, he checked behind and in both directions before turning onto the highway. "If we see any cars coming, I want both of you to duck. Hopefully, we'll be far from here before there's an APB on me."

He glanced at Claire. "Now tell us why we had to hurry."

She turned in her seat, facing both Brad and Candy and explained about the men at the cabin. "You called when he was about halfway back to the main trail."

"So, he might have heard me drive in."

"I don't know, but I didn't want to stay there long enough to find out."

"Let's hope they don't realize for a while I was the one who picked you up."

Candy sat forward. "Why not?"

"Because then they'll be looking for my truck, too."

A car approached from around a curve a half mile ahead.

"All right, ladies. Time to hide."

Candy dropped to the seat and stretched out. Claire shoved the shoulder harness off her shoulder, tipped sideways and dropped her head onto Brad's thigh.

It was more intimate than he expected. His knuckles turned white as he tightened his grip on the steering wheel. He wondered if they'd been alone, would he have been able to hold back from touching her. They were on the run, and Jeffery's funeral had been that day; it wasn't the time to think this way.

"Two more cars coming." In the rearview mirror, the third car disappeared around a curve. He waited a few seconds longer than necessary because he didn't want Claire's head leaving his lap.

"All clear." Both women sat up.

The women didn't seem as tense as him. Maybe they hid it better. Maybe they trusted him too much to protect them. So much could still go wrong.

A few miles after crossing into the next county, Brad turned into the half full parking lot at a discount store. He angled into a space between two other trucks near the front so his would blend in, and turned sideways in his seat. "You two wait here. I'll get a phone for Candy and be right out."

"Can I come, too?" Claire asked. "I had to leave all my clothes behind."

Brad shook his head. "Your face has been plastered everywhere. You'd be recognized for sure." He removed a receipt and pen from the glove box. "Why don't you write down some essentials and I'll see what I can do?"

She sighed. "All right." She scribbled on the paper and handed it back to Brad.

"I'm leaving the keys in the ignition. If anything seems wrong, get out of here fast."

"Brad." There was a hint of a whine in her voice.

"I don't think anything is going to happen, but we need to be prepared."

****

"You care about him, don't you?" Candy asked.

"I've known him since I was five. Of course I care about him."

"You know I don't mean it like that. You love him."

"Umm." It was too new. She couldn't admit it. She wasn't even sure if she did love him that way.

"He loves you, too."

Claire raised her brows. "Why do you think that?"

Candy's face softened. "It's the way he talks about you. How he's working so hard to save you. How he looks at you when you're not looking at him."

"Ah, thanks, Candy. But I think it's only that he's worried about me." She wanted what Candy said to be true. If only it wasn't the wrong time. The guilt over not believing Jeffery ate at her. Maybe he'd still be alive if she'd stayed with him, trusted him. Maybe Brad couldn't love her with how she'd rejected his best friend.

Claire checked her watch and scanned the parking lot. Her heart skipped a beat and she jolted back.

Candy turned around. "What is it?"

"Duck. A police car drove in." They dove down, out of sight.

Candy's voice shook. "I hope they're picking up a shoplifter."

Chapter 12

Brad opened the door, and Claire's head snapped up from the seat, her eyes huge. She closed them, dropped her head and her shoulders sagged.

She lifted her head. "Did you see the police? Why are they here?"

He slid into the seat and shook his head. "No idea. I saw the police car when I came out, but nobody inside. I don't think it's for us."

He assembled the cell phone, plugged the charger into it and the other end into power, and set it on the seat. Then started the truck and headed to the farthest exit before turning onto the road. After a few blocks, he told them they could sit up.

Silence reigned. Claire stared out the back window.

Brad glanced in the rear view mirror, then at Claire. "He didn't follow us. Relax."

She turned forward, dropped against the seatback and closed her eyes.

He rubbed her arm, causing her to jump and stare at him. He slid his hand down to hers and laced their fingers. "Everything's going to be okay. After we drop Candy, we'll hammer out the details for tomorrow."

Brad's shoulders eased a little when he turned into the bus station parking lot. There were no police cars. He hadn't wanted to worry the women any more than necessary. He unplugged Candy's new phone from the power and punched in his and Claire's burner cell phone numbers, then handed it to her. "I have my and Claire's numbers programmed into it. Don't call anyone else. Give one of your friends a call and see if you can visit. Then you can call back after we get your ticket."

"All right." She opened her purse and extracted a paper. She dialed the first one. "Ugh. Voicemail." She hung up without leaving a message and tried the other number. She talked for fifteen minutes to her friend and hung up.

"We're all set."

He lifted his eyebrows. "Is this guy an old boyfriend?"

"No. Jim was a friend of a guy I dated when I was in college. We hit it off and kept in touch."

"He sounds like a good choice for you to hide with. Is it all right you're missing the last two days at the academy before your break?" He hoped it would be cleared up before she missed any more time.

"It's fine. I'll catch up."

He nodded. "Let's see about getting you to your friend."

They headed inside and Candy scanned the signs and told them which bus station was the closest to Jim.

Brad bought a ticket and led them to the street and surveyed the line of buildings. "We've got two hours to kill, let's get something to eat."

They made their way to a diner at the end of the block and entered.

A waitress smiled. "Welcome, folks. Sit where you want." She turned back to an elderly couple, her pen poised over a pad.

He scanned the room. Only three tables were occupied, so he chose the corner farthest from them all. He positioned himself so he could watch activity through the window and in the room, and see anyone entering the door. He had Claire sit with her back to the room. She was more exposed than he was comfortable with. Maybe he should have gotten sandwiches and had them eat in the truck.

He stretched across the table, startling her when he ran his hands through her hair, leaving it partially covering her face. "When you order, keep your eyes on the menu. Hopefully, the waitress won't notice you."

The menus were tucked between the napkin holder and a rack holding condiments. He plucked them out, giving one to each woman and took one for himself. He relaxed a little when Claire tipped her head forward, studying the selection.

The waitress arrived with glasses of water, and pulled out her pad and pen. "What can I get you?" She gazed at Candy.

"I'll have a BLT with fries and a Coke."

"And you, miss?"

Claire pointed to an item on the page. "I'll have a chicken club, fries and Coke."

Well done, Claire.

The waitress glanced at the menu, wrote and raised her brows at Brad.

"Cheese burger, fries and a coke."

"It'll be just a few minutes." She hurried away.

They talked through their meal and Brad insisted they order dessert so they could stay longer in the restaurant.

He glanced at his watch as Claire sat her fork next to the half finished apple pie.

"Time to get out of here." He flipped over the check the waitress left with the desserts, dropped money on it, and stood.

They filed out the door and headed to Brad's truck, stopping to pick up Candy's bag.

Claire hugged Candy. "Be careful and call if anything seems weird."

"I will."

Brad took Candy's hand in both of his and pressed

money into her palm.

"Brad, no. I have cash."

"I want to make sure you won't have to use any cards, so take it."

She stared at their joined hands for several seconds, then closed her fingers around the money. "Okay."

They strolled to the bus. Candy got on and took a seat about a third of the way back, waving from the window. They waved back and the bus drove off.

Claire caught her lip between her teeth. "I hope she stays safe."

He put his arm around her shoulder. "She will."

She glanced up at him. "Now what?"

"We head to the state capital. Tomorrow we'll see the state attorney general."

Her eyebrows rose. "Do you think he'll see us?"

"Yeah, with what we've got, he'll see us."

"I sure hope so."

****

They gained the outskirts of the capital a little after nine. Since dinner with Candy had been early, Claire was glad when Brad turned into the drive-through of a fast food restaurant. They ate as he searched for a place to stay. He passed two chain motels before pulling into the lot of a small independent. Four cars sat, spaced out, in front of some of the units. Probably six more were empty.

"Stay here while I register." He got out of the truck and returned several minutes later. "I only got one room because we have to watch our cash."

A shared room? A shared bed? She wasn't sure what she wanted or if she was ready.

He drove to the backside of the building where two cars

already occupied spaces near the end. "I told him I didn't want to hear road noise. I hope the police don't cruise through here checking license plates."

He backed into the space in front of unit fifteen and Claire jumped out, clasping her purse and bag of clothes. He grabbed his duffle bag from the back floor, and she followed him to the door, waited for him to open it, then stepped in and scanned the room. She let out a breath at the sight of two beds in the small space. No decision about that tonight.

A feint floral odor tickled her nose. No flowers graced the room. It must have been a room deodorizer. The carpet was worn but reasonably clean. An old TV sat on a pressed board dresser. A sagging desk with a chair sat beside it. She peeked into the a clean bathroom to find thin towels. Not what she would have chosen, but perfect for a hideout. And no worse than the cabin, but that she was used to.

Brad dropped his bag on the chair and turned on the TV. A reporter described flooding in a town fifty miles north of them.

She set her bag and purse beside his and entered the bathroom. She returned as Brad shuffled through his bag, laptop on the bed closest to the door.

She sat on the other bed, scooted up to lean against the headboard and watched him as the newscaster droned. Jeffery's name caught her attention and she stared in pain at the screen. Video footage showed people leaving the church Jeffery's parents attended. The announcer stated people were leaving the funeral of officer Jeffery Dickens.

Brad picked up the remote control.

"No, leave it on."

The reporter reminded people Deputy Dickens had been gunned down in a parking lot the previous week and his killer was still free. They showed Claire's picture and she shivered. Her friends and acquaintances would know she couldn't kill anyone, let alone Jeffery. She didn't know why nobody questioned the sheriff's story. But hers didn't make any more.

She turned away from the screen and regarded him. "Do you think they'll arrest me tomorrow?"

"I hope not. I think once the AG hears all the facts, he'll want to protect you. Do you want to stay here while I go?"

Thoughts jumbled through her head. She bit her lip. "I don't know. I want to go and help you convince him of the truth, but I don't want him to arrest me while he's verifying our story. I'd have less of a chance protecting myself than those men who died in custody."

He sat beside her. "I don't know what to tell you."

She took a deep breath and let it out with a huff. "I'm going to stay here tomorrow. I don't think I can risk it until we know how the AG responds." She was grateful the decision was hers.

He stood. "I'm going to go pick up something for tomorrow's breakfast."

He took two steps toward the door when she spoke. "Can you get me a book to read? If I'm going to be stuck here for who knows how long, I don't want to have just the TV for company."

"Sure." He studied her. "You still like murder mysteries?"

"Yeah. I'm not sure I will once we're done with all this."

When he returned, he lifted one bag. "Muffins for breakfast. The other has peanut butter, jam and bread for lunch. And a couple apples."

"Oh, yum," Claire said.

"I didn't have much of a choice for something that wouldn't need refrigeration."

She fished a small notebook from her purse. "Ok, let's plan what you're going to tell the AG."

They worked for a couple of hours hashing and rehashing the details until they were both satisfied. Brad would use labeled pictures for his ticket into the office. From there, he'd give a summary of the details and hope the AG would want to read through the rest of their information.

Brad stretched. Claire craved to touch his muscular chest without the hindrance of his shirt. She lowered her gaze, but the image was already burned in her head.

He stifled a yawn. "I've got to get some sleep if I'm going to make sense tomorrow."

"I'm tired, too." After using the bathroom to change into a t-shirt, she climbed into the bed farthest from the door. A few minutes later, Brad approached wearing only his boxers. It'd been a couple years since she'd seen him in swim trunks and she hadn't been affected like she was now. She wanted to run her hands up his biceps, slide them across his chest, feel his heartbeat quicken. She closed her eyes, concentrated on slowing her breathing and pretended she was asleep. Surprisingly, it didn't take long to fall asleep.

Chapter 13

Claire flowed up through the layers of sleep. A strip of early morning light slanted across her pillow. She slid the pillow back to avoid the light. Of course, they had to be on the east side of the building.

Without the light in her eyes, she could see Brad in the other bed. The blanket had slipped to his waist, revealing his tanned chest. Those muscles she'd touched a few times were more impressive without fabric and would be even better to stroke. She bunched up the blanket in her fist. She had a vision of herself scooting out of her bed, sliding under his sheet and running her hand all over his chest. He would awaken, smile, and kiss her.

She closed her eyes and stifled a groan, ran a hand down her face and opened her eyes again.

Brad watched her.

She caught her breath, wondering if that expression meant he was having the same thoughts. Her mouth became a desert and she licked her lips.

He gave her a small smile. "Morning, Claire." His voice was soft and gruff. He shifted to the edge of the bed.

"G'morning, Brad."

He sat up, shoved his covers away and half stood.

Her gaze found his chest and dipped down to his boxers. She closed her eyes. Was that a morning thing or was he thinking about her, way more than friendly? Her eyes snapped open when his breath touched her face. How could a face be serious and sexy at the same time?

He ran a finger down her cheek. "I want to make love to you."

She forgot to breathe for several seconds, and then she could only draw in shallow breaths. Was he afraid it would be their last chance? Maybe it was. He could be arrested for helping a fugitive or because of whatever evidence Crowley planted. She could be arrested or put in protective custody. The day might not unfold the way they hoped.

He wanted to do exactly what she'd dreamed of them doing. But dreaming and doing were two different things. Maybe she wasn't ready for this.

The sparkle left his eyes and he started to stand. She'd taken too long to make up her mind, and he'd given up. She snatched his hand. "Me, too."

His sexy smile melted her. She was glad he hadn't used that weapon earlier. She lifted the blanket and slid away from him.

He opened the nightstand drawer and plucked a condom from it.

"You were prepared."

He shrugged and gave her that sexy smile. "I hoped."

She didn't know if these smiles were different, or if she saw them differently.

He turned away from her, dropped his boxers, and sat on the bed, then twisted to face her as he slipped in beside her.

He gave her quick little kisses. They were sweet, but she wanted more. She tunneled her fingers into his hair and held his head still as she tickled his lips with her tongue. He groaned and deepened the kiss. Finally.

His hand slipped under her shirt and ran up her spine.

A shiver followed his hand, making her squirm, making her need more.

He pulled her shirt up, and she lifted for him to remove it. He rolled, covering one breast with his body, a knee between hers.

Her body heated. She skimmed one hand up his side to his shoulder and imbedded the other in his hair. He was really there with her. It wasn't a fantasy this time.

His hand skimmed up her ribs and over her breast. She moaned when a finger swirled around her nipple. He rolled it between his thumb and finger and she arched, bringing a more intimate contact with his thigh. She wrapped her arm over his waist. "More."

This was happening. It wasn't a dream like so many she'd had about him in the cabin. Maybe they shouldn't be doing this, but she couldn't think of anything she needed more right now. When she wasn't thinking about her guilt over Jeffery or getting out of this predicament, her thoughts and imagination centered on Brad.

He slid down and kissed her other breast. He licked, nibbled and sucked. His hand slipped into her panties.

She surged up. "Brad!" It'd been so long, she'd almost forgotten how good it could be.

She lifted as he slid her panties down and when they reached her ankles, she kicked them off. All thoughts fled except how he seemed to know exactly what to do to make her scream.

****

Hour or long minutes could have passed. Brad didn't know. Making love with Claire had been better than any fantasy he'd had. He loved her, and his heart expanded even more as they made love for the first time. Her body warmed his side and her head rested on his chest. He buried his nose in her hair, enjoying her scent mixed with the shampoo. His heart still beat too fast.

She'd always been out of reach, so he'd lived his own

life and searched for his own woman. It never worked out. He'd even been accused of not being able to love, but it was only that he already loved and no one else measured up. He'd accepted he'd probably die an old bachelor. A small pang of guilt tweaked him over what they'd done, but Jeffery wouldn't have wanted Claire to remain alone. He'd want Brad to take care of her if he couldn't.

She kissed his chest and snuggled closer.

He'd get Claire out of this trouble and then they could spend the rest of their lives together. He tightened his arm around her.

It was probably a bad time to ask, but he'd wondered for years. Maybe he didn't even want the answer. He should leave it alone, but once the question popped into his brain, he plunged ahead. "Uh, Claire, why did you choose Jeffery?"

She lifted her head, raised her eyebrows, and bit her lip. "Um, I didn't."

He tipped his head and frowned, not expecting a non-answer.

She dropped her head back down. "When we were about sixteen, I realized I was in love with both of you. I don't know when friendship turned into that kind of love. I even had sexual fantasies about both of you." Her cheeks turned an adorable shade of pink.

"Together?" he teased.

She whipped her head up and stared at him with wide-open eyes. "What? No! I was a naive teen who didn't date."

She put her head back on his chest. "Anyway, there was no way I could have chosen."

What did that mean? She had chosen. Jeffery.

****

She shrugged. "It was just that Jeffery was the first to

ask me out." She remembered it so well. They were seventeen. The junior prom was getting closer. No one had asked her to go. In fact, she'd never had a date. It wasn't that she didn't talk to guys. She talked to a lot of them in and out of class. She'd thought there was something wrong with her. She'd wanted Jeffery or Brad to ask her, but at that point, she would have accepted any offer. She didn't want to be among the girls not going. Then Jeffery shyly asked if she wanted to go with him. It was kind of funny because he was never shy with her. She figured he was afraid she'd refuse.

She returned to the present as Brad said, "Then I backed off."

"Yeah, I didn't see much of you after that." She hadn't realized her relationship with one friend would change when she accepted a date from the other. They'd still been friends but it hadn't been the same anymore. She'd missed him, the way it used to be. It started to seem more like he was only Jeffery's friend. Even at the cabin after that, he'd been distant.

She cupped his cheek.

He turned and kissed her hand. "I had trouble dealing with seeing the two of you together as a couple."

She kissed him.

He stared over her shoulder. "Sometimes I told myself, if I had asked you out first, you'd be with me."

"You're probably right."

His stomach clench under her hand. Maybe she shouldn't have told him. It really didn't reflect well on her. In the end, she'd let them choose. She didn't regret it. She'd loved Jeffery. They'd had a good marriage until...the misunderstanding.

****

He and Jeffery had made a pact to protect Claire from the wrong type of guys. It turned out, the two of them had protected her so well, no one dared to ask her out. He hadn't wanted her to go out with other guys.

He'd been considering asking her out himself, but it would change things between them. If she said no, would they still be friends? If she said yes, would Jeffery become a fifth wheel? If they started dating and broke up, would they lose their friendship? Before he'd come to a decision, Jeffery had asked her out and he was left to love her from afar.

And it had changed things. He'd never resented Jeffery. He was glad she was happy with one of them, even if it wasn't him.

Now she was his.

Then guilt overtook him. It was only because his best friend was dead he had this chance with Claire. Maybe he didn't deserve her. Would she have been better off if he and Jeffery had let other guys date her?

Claire frowned. "What's wrong?"

He shook his head. "Nothing. Just old memories that need to stay old." He kissed her. "I can't wait until I get back to you. But now, I've got a lot to do and it's a later start than I intended." He grinned and kissed her again. "Not that I'm complaining." With regret, he climbed out of bed, wishing he didn't have to leave her so soon after their first time.

****

Claire sat up, drew the covers over her knees, and snugged them to her chest, wrapping her arms around them. He seemed stiff as he walked to the bathroom. It didn't detract from the great view. She sighed. A change had overtaken him in the last few minutes. She didn't know what had caused it, and hoped he didn't regret what they'd done.

101

She didn't. Their first time making love. It was better than any of her fantasies. Of course, most had been in her teens, but the few from the past week still weren't as good as the real thing. She grinned. Now she had a whole slew of new fantasy material.

She got up and slipped her arms into Brad's shirt, but left it unbuttoned. It came halfway to her knees. She opened her bag of clothes. There were two t-shirts, one red, one yellow. She held up a pair of black yoga pants, which weren't the sweat pants she'd asked for, tossed them on the bed with the red shirt. She ripped open a package of bikini panties, tossed one pair on the bed. Next, she found a lacy, pale pink bra. She'd never bought such a daring, wispy thing, but she was stuck with it. Had he planned on seeing her in it or just imagining it?

"I think that will look hot on you."

She spun around and one side of the shirt flew back.

"But, not as sexy as my shirt." He gave her a one sided smiled that tripped her heart.

After what they'd done, how could a smile make her want to crawl back into bed with him? Her face heated and she drew the edges of the shirt together.

"Aw, don't spoil it."

She couldn't take her eyes off his grin as he stalked toward her. She'd never seen this playful side of him before, but liked it. The bra dropped to the floor as he stopped in front of her. One hand held the too small towel around his waist that was getting smaller by the second. He slipped the other hand inside the shirt and cupped her breast. She placed her hand on his still damp chest.

"I wish I could stay." He kissed her. She wrapped her arms around his neck and tugged him closer. He let go of his towel, and it stayed pressed between them, as his arms circled her.

"You're going to have to take my shirt off," he whispered. "It's the only dress shirt I have with me."

Claire nodded, letting it slide down her arms. He grabbed it before it landed in a heap on the floor, and his towel slipped away.

Both of them naked and she couldn't act on it. At least one part of his body wanted to as much as she did.

He presented his back as he put on the shirt, then swiftly donned the rest of his clothes.

Was he afraid he'd give in if he kept watching her? She stifled a giggle.

Once again, he faced her. He leaned in, letting only his lips touch hers. "I'm going to think of you like this all day. I better not embarrass myself." He stepped back. "I'm paying for another night here. Stay inside."

He gave her a quick kiss. She loved how he couldn't stop kissing her, but wished they lasted longer.

"Hopefully, I'll have good news when I see you next." He slipped out the door, shaking the doorknob after closing it, making sure it was locked.

She slid the chain into place.

Without an appointment, the AG might not see Brad. And if he did, she hoped he'd believe their evidence. She already worried, and he'd left minutes ago. She'd never make it through the next few hours.

Chapter 14

Brad shifted in his chair as he stared at the Attorney General's middle-aged secretary, Jeanie. He'd pinned everything on the envelope sitting on her spotless desk.

On each picture, he'd written a description of the scene. The AG could send him away without opening it, never finding out he had a dirty agent. He might not care that Agent Matt Richards appeared to be doing something illegal. The weight of the flash drive in his pocket also weighed on his spirit. He hoped he'd get a chance to show his evidence. The AG had to be curious enough to invite him in. Had to be. Otherwise, it was hopeless. He and Claire would still be alone and could both die.

He shifted again in his chair.

Every few minutes Jeanie stopped typing as her gaze darted to the phone. A call rang in and she answered.

No! He didn't want to wait even longer.

She talked for a minute, hung up and started typing again. Finally, she glanced his way and stood, picked up the envelope and disappeared behind a door.

He tensed. This was it. Either he'd get to present their evidence or he'd have to find another way to clear Claire. There was also the chance an APB had gone out on him, and the AG had requested agents to come arrest him. He tapped his foot. How long before he got his answer?

The moment the door cracked open, he jumped to his feet.

Jeanie stepped into the room. "You can go in now."

Brad sucked in a deep breath and stood. "Thank you." Half the battle was won. Maybe a third.

She closed the door, sealing him inside. For a second, his imaginings trapped him, waiting for someone to take him away in handcuffs.

He strode to the desk with a feigned confidence, and held out his hand. "Detective Brad Hayes, sir."

The AG stood eye level with Brad, giving him a firm handshake. "Jacob Purcell. Have a seat." Purcell's rolled up sleeves suggested he was willing to tackle a tough case.

They sat and Purcell rubbed his chin. "Your pictures intrigued me. Are you trying to tell me I have a dirty agent on my hands?"

"That's how it looks to me, sir. Although, that agent and my sheriff are trying to turn me into the guilty party."

Purcell leaned forward, his face stern. "Tell me what you've got, Detective Hayes." He slapped his hand on the photos. "This isn't enough for me to pursue it."

"Brad, please." He nodded toward the photos. "Those were my ticket in. I've got more." Purcell seemed willing to listen. Brad hoped that after he presented his evidence, it would be enough. He'd been through this with Richards, and dug a deeper hole. He hoped the corruption didn't go this far up the chain.

Brad took a calming breath. "I got dragged into this the night Sheriff Dean Crowley shot his deputy, my best friend, Jeffery Dickens."

"I know that Deputy Dickens was shot, but I thought his ex-wife killed him and shot Sheriff Crowley."

"That's what Crowley said, but I have a witness who says Crowley shot Jeffery and pointed his gun at Jeffery's ex, but she shot first."

Purcell nodded. "Continue."

Brad told everything they were sure of and some things

they'd guessed. He finished with, "I have more pictures, Jeffery's journal of his investigation and a file of purchases and sales of contraband."

Purcell's eyebrows pinched together. "I find it hard to believe Matt Richards is involved in this. I've worked with him. He seems like an honest guy. Maybe he's working undercover, although I don't know about it."

Brad pointed at the picture he'd written on. "That would have been the perfect setup to arrest Crowley. How much more evidence would he have needed? Richards also showed up alone at Jeffery's house after dark. I assumed he was looking for something. If he was legitimate, he would have gone there during the day with a search warrant."

Purcell pursed his lips. "All right. Show me what you've got."

Brad rounded Purcell's desk, opened his laptop, then fished the flash drive out of his pocket. Half a minute later, he displayed the first of the pictures they'd selected.

"This is the first car Jeffery saw with guns in the trunk." He continued through a selection of pictures, giving descriptions where needed. At the end, Purcell opened the journal.

"I'll let you read that." Brad sat back in the chair and crossed his ankle over his knee.

Purcell's expression changed as he read, but Brad wasn't sure if it was surprise or disbelief. His gaze stopped scanning, but Purcell's eyes never left the page. Brad hoped he was trying to fit everything together, and coming up with the same conclusion Claire and he had.

Purcell had to see it like they did. The AG hadn't known Jeffery, wouldn't know he'd never turn. He did know Richards, so it would be harder to accept his own man was dirty.

The longer Brad waited, the tighter his shoulders tensed,

the more worried he became that he hadn't succeeded. He couldn't wait another minute.

Purcell jabbed the intercom button. "Jeanie?"

Brad hunched forward. Purcell's response would have been nice before calling his secretary. He didn't know if he was believed or if he should try to escape the building. Were the AG's men nearby?

"Yes, sir?"

"Can you bring in two coffees?" He glanced at Brad. "Black?"

Brad nodded and sat back, his shoulders relaxed, the tension in his stomach uncoiled.

"Both black."

"Coming right up."

"What do you think, sir?"

"Let's wait for the coffee."

Good idea not to trust the secretary either. Anything she might catch them discussing would be sensitive.

Jeanie bustled in with two steaming white ceramic mugs. The smell of coffee heightened his senses.

Jeanie exited and Purcell took a sip from his cup. "I agree with you. I think Crowley and Richards are both bad cops. Dickens and Miller were killed to keep it quiet, as well as the two jailed drivers." He leaned back, put his elbows on the armrests and steepled his fingers. "Now, to catch them in the act."

Brad smiled. "I have a plan."

Purcell tipped his head. "Go ahead."

Brad walked around the desk again. He shifted the mug to his left hand and opened another document on his laptop. "This is the spreadsheet. See how the dates are mostly one week apart. It's always a Monday. I think Richards procures the guns over the weekend and wants to get rid of them ASAP. If you have someone watching him starting Friday night, you could find where the guns are coming from. Then follow either him or Crowley on Monday and catch them both in the act."

"I can put someone on him Friday and see if he goes anywhere. Now about your witness and Dickens' ex-wife."

Brad stiffened. "What about them?" He should be able to trust the AG, but Richards had played like he was working with Brad. There was no telling who else in the Attorney General's office might be dirty.

"I think we should bring them in and put them under protection."

"I'm not going to do that."

Purcell's eyebrows rose and he tipped his head back. "You don't trust me?"

Brad tapped his chest. "The only one I trust is me. You trusted Richards before talking to me this morning. Can you guarantee whoever you call would protect them?"

Purcell made a fist and blew out a breath. "You may be right. I have to clean house. I don't like it, but I'll let you continue to protect them."

"Thank you, sir."

Purcell propelled his chair back. "Let me get this investigation moving. I'll go outside my department."

"I'd like to be kept informed."

The AG studied him. A lot of thoughts must have tumbled through the man's head, but Brad had no idea what decision he'd make. Brad was giving his trust because he didn't have another choice. There was still a risk for Claire if this didn't work as planned. He and Claire could run, but they'd spend their lives hiding. And there was still the risk to Candy.

Purcell gave a curt nod. "I'll let you know if anything happens Friday night."

Brad gave him the number of his prepaid cell phone.

Purcell handed him a card with his private number. Brad held out his hand. "Thank you for seeing me. I'd like to be in on the arrest on Monday if Friday pans out."

Purcell shook Brad's hand. "You deserve to be. I'll see what I can do."

Chapter 15

Claire glanced at the clock for the hundredth, maybe thousandth time. A few minutes had passed since the last time she'd checked. For a moment, she wished she was sitting beside Brad, so she'd know what was happening. She jumped up and flung her book on the bed. She had no idea what she'd read anyway. It was the wisest decision to stay behind, but right now, it left her edgy.

She paced to the door and then the far wall, and back again. Halfway to the wall again, a knock had her spinning around. Her heart kicked up its pace, and her throat tightened. It seemed too early for Brad. It could be someone there to arrest her. Or kill her. Would a killer knock? Probably. She sighed in relief at Brad's voice. Rushing to the door, she opened it and hauled him in.

He pushed the door closed and rammed home the security chain. "You should have stayed behind the door, so no one could see you."

"Sorry, I was just so relieved it was you."

She wrapped her arms around him in a bear hug. "I missed you. I worried. It feels like the whole world is against us." She stepped back, trying to read his face. "How did it go? Did you get in?"

Brad grabbed her hand and led her to the nearest bed. "Let's sit down, and I'll tell you all about it."

"So, he did see you." There wouldn't be much to tell if he hadn't.

He scooted up to the headboard and dragged Claire to

his side. She leaned against his arm and entwined her fingers with his.

He kissed the top of her head. "Yes. He was on the phone and I had to wait forever for the secretary to take him the envelope. I was on pins and needles until she returned and invited me in."

While Brad described the details of his visit, Claire stared at their hands. It had to be over soon, but so much could still go wrong. It could turn out the best way possible, but Jeffery would still be dead. There was a hole in their lives that would take a long time to heal.

"Do you think he believed you?"

"Yes. I can't see how he wouldn't. We don't have everything we need, but there's enough to show both Crowley and Richards are dirty cops. Now it's a matter of waiting until they do another run."

"I hope it's soon." She sighed. Richards or Crowley could still find them before getting caught in the trap.

"What?" Brad feigned a hurt expression. "You don't want to be hidden away with me?"

She touched his cheek. "I love being hidden away with you. I just don't like the reason." Her lips skimmed his. "There are so many better reasons to be hidden away."

"Speaking of staying hidden, I found a nicer motel to stay at tomorrow."

She scanned the room. "You mean we have to leave this love nest?"

"Anywhere you are is my love nest."

He gripped the bottom of her shirt and Claire lifted her arms to help him remove it. He tossed it on the other bed and ran a finger along the lacey, pink edge of her bra.

"Pink's not my usual color." She shivered.

"I think it's perfect." He ran his hand over the bra and cupped her. His lips returned to hers as she unbuttoned his shirt. He shrugged out of it and slid them down the bed.

He leaned in to kiss her again, then dropped onto his back, groaning. "I was in such a rush to get back to you, I forgot to buy condoms."

Claire ran her fingers down his chest, tipped her head down and closed her eyes. "I'm not sure we need them."

He put his hand over hers. "You're on birth control?"

Eyes still closed, she shook her head. She'd pushed the pain away for months. There'd been no reason to think of children.

He tipped her head up and she opened her eyes, meeting his frown.

"What is it?"

"Jeffery and I tried for almost a year to have a baby. We had an appointment with a fertility specialist, but after...that woman, I cancelled it."

"It might not be you."

She shrugged. No, she didn't know for sure, but her heart ached with the emptiness like it was her fault.

He kissed her again. "I love you no matter what." He stripped them of their remaining clothing.

****

Much later, Claire woke with her head on Brad's shoulder, her leg tangled with his and her hand curled on his stomach. She straightened her fingers and slid them up to the hair on his chest. She lifted one finger and wiggled it back and forth, tickling the pad with the curly hair. Warmth filled her heart as the last words Brad said before they made love repeated in her head. Did he love her like they were a couple? Or was this some kind of friends with benefits thing?

She hadn't expected them to get together like this. Brad had kept his distance after she and Jeffery separated. Maybe he blamed her for the breakup. And, in a way, she was responsible.

If they had stayed together, Jeffery probably would have confided in her about his investigation long ago. If he had, he might be alive today. Did that make her partially responsible for his death as well?

She sighed. Brad's hand threaded through her hair. "What's wrong?"

She touched her lips to his chest, then focused on his eyes. "I want all this to be over."

He scrunched his eyes. "All of it?"

She wiggled higher to have better access to his mouth and kissed him. "Well, the scary, dangerous parts. You, I'll hold onto." She pressed her lips to his and he wrapped his other arm around her and tugged her over him. She stretched back and studied him. "Brad?" She took a deep breath and let it out.

"Hmm?"

"Do you think I'm partially responsible for Jeffery's death because I wasn't there for him when he needed to talk?"

His arm tightened around her. "Claire, no! Crowley is responsible. Jeffery should have come to me as soon as he suspected Crowley. There's no way you could have known things weren't the way they appeared."

He put his finger under her chin and lifted it a bit. "Do you feel guilty we're together like this?"

She shook her head. "No. I think Jeffery would want us together since he can't be here to take care of me." She wagged her forefinger at him. "Not that I need it. Well, usually. But, you know he'd say that."

"He did," Brad whispered.

"What?"

"A couple months ago, Jeffery said, 'If anything

113

happens to me, take care of Claire.' I think he knew he was in trouble, and he still didn't talk to me about it. I wish I'd realized at the time what he was telling me."

"I divorced him and he still wanted to make sure I was taken care of?" He'd loved her so much and she'd thrown it away. "Umm." She waved her hand back and forth between them. "We aren't together like this because of what Jeffery said, are we?"

In a flurry, he rolled over so she was under him. Her yelp was cut off when his lips claimed hers. He lifted his head. "Does that feel like we're only together because Jeffery asked me to take care of you?"

She shook her head.

"I love you. I can't think of a time I didn't. This is the kind of love a man has for a woman, not a sister. Don't question it," he said in a stern voice.

She grinned and wrapped her arms around his neck. "I won't." She nipped his lip then dropped her head to the pillow. "I love you." The way his eyes lit up at her declaration, gave her the feeling her heart had been hugged. She kissed him again and giggled when her stomach growled.

He kissed her tummy. "All right. I'll feed you."

"There's peanut butter and jam."

"I think we can do better than that. I saw a Chinese restaurant not far from here. I'll go pick something up." He pushed up onto his knees and towered over her. He ran a finger from her neck, down between her breasts, to her navel. "I wouldn't mind if you still showed lots of skin when I get back."

She sat up, as he got off the bed and put his clothes on. After he slipped out the door, she got out of bed and dressed. He was not going to find her naked in bed when he got back. She was starved and food would be forgotten if she wasn't dressed.

Chapter 16

They had a few hours to kill before check in time at the next motel, so Brad suggested a hike on a trail about an hour away. It had been remote enough they'd only passed a couple people on the trail. Each time, she kept her face hidden. Their troubles had been miles away, allowing Claire to relax as she hadn't been able to in days. The fresh air had been wonderful.

She tensed as they past into the city limits. All the worry and fear rushed back. "Thanks, Brad. It was nice getting away. For a short time, I forgot about all our troubles for a while."

He touched her cheek. "Are you tired?"

"Not tired. Worn out from the hike, but in a good way."

"After we're settled into the room, I'll pick up some food." Brad got out of the truck and entered the office. He returned five minutes later with a key in his hand. He drove to the end of the building. Pine trees lined the edge of the road, hiding the end of the motel.

It hadn't been hard that morning to pack so few pieces of clothing and even easier to gather their bags. Brad checked the parking lot and opened his truck door, motioning Claire to get out. She kept her head down so her hair obscured her face while he opened the motel room door.

She surveyed the room. "This is better than the last one." She turned from the king sized bed. "I guess we don't need two beds anymore." Now she was familiar with that expression in his eyes and her heart kicked up a notch in anticipation. A small table with two chairs sat in front of the window. At least they'd be more comfortable while eating. She took a few steps to the bathroom and peeked in. "I think I'll shower while you're gone. That should refresh me."

Brad kissed her and it was hard letting him go. "I shouldn't be long."

She picked up the bag and emptied it on the bed. Such a pathetic wardrobe. She'd rinsed out her underwear and shirts the night before. They'd still been damp in the morning, but were dry now. She'd have to do the same with the shirt she wore. She'd gotten warm on the hike and the cloth stuck on her arms as she tugged it off.

A key jiggled in the lock. Brad must have forgotten something. She waited for him to come in and wondered why he didn't knock. Maybe the key was stuck. She took three steps toward the door when it opened and a man with a ski mask over his face stepped in and closed it. She gasped and held the shirt up to cover herself.

The man pointed a gun at her. "Put the shirt on. You're coming with me."

Claire gaped for several seconds. Every hour she'd been in the cabin, she expected someone to show up at the door and take her away. The more miles they'd driven, she'd relaxed, began to think they wouldn't be found unless they wanted to be. Brad had been so sure no one had followed them.

"H-how did you find me?"

"I planted a tracker on Hayes' truck while he was in the church. Now get your shirt on or you'll go like that."

This man hadn't been at Jeffery's funeral, so he was an outsider. She turned her back, struggled with shaky hands to pull her shirt over her head and turned to face him. She was almost surprised he hadn't shot her. There must be a reason to keep her alive.

"Now give me your cell phone."

"M-my phone?"

"Yeah, you want to be able to call lover boy later, don't you?"

She was a lure to trap Brad. She'd rather Brad never find her again than this man kill him. And probably kill her right after.

She picked up her purse from the bed. Hopefully, he'd give her enough time. The man was beside her in an instant and snatched it away.

"My phone is in my purse." He'd taken her only chance to get away. She wrapped her arms around herself and wiped her damp palms on her hips.

"Yeah, but what else is in there?" He held the purse strap with his gun hand and rummaged in it with the other. He extracted her gun. "Like this." He shoved the gun into his pants pocket. He found her phone and put it into his shirt pocket, then dropped her purse on the bed. Half the contents spilled out. He waved toward the door with the gun. "Now let's go."

"Can I put my shoes on?" If she delayed, maybe Brad would get back. But, she couldn't delay too long because she didn't know if it mattered to this guy if she lived.

He huffed. "Be quick about it."

Even with shaky fingers, she slipped on and tied her shoes in too little time. She crept to the door, not knowing what else she could do. A long time ago, she'd taken some self-defense training, but anything she'd learned had deserted her. Her life would probably be only as long as it took to get Brad. She stopped once they stepped outside.

"That car there." He pointed to a dark blue sedan. She'd been around law enforcement enough to recognize an unmarked police car. "We're getting in the passenger side and you're going to slide over to the driver's seat." Once she was behind the wheel, he handed her the keys, but they slipped from her fingers.

"Damn, woman!" He picked them up, jammed them into the ignition and started the car. "Back out. Go left onto the road."

Maybe she could put the car in drive and crash it into the building. He'd probably hit her before she'd gone a foot. Or shoot her.

She had no idea how long Brad had been gone. He could drive in before they left the parking lot. But he didn't.

She sat forward in the seat, her back stiff. Every time she tried speeding up, he told her to slow down and stuck the gun in her side. No getting pulled over. He directed each turn as she approached it. She memorized their route in hopes she could escape and find her way back to help.

****

Brad opened the door and walked into the motel room. A quiet emptiness encased him. Something was wrong.

"Claire?"

He dropped his bags on the table beside the door when he noticed her purse spilled on the bed. He dug through it. Her phone and gun were gone. How did they find her? Who found her?

He called her number, not expecting her to answer, and left a message.

Cold invaded him and his heart pounded. Claire's life had been in danger all along. He should have been more careful. It couldn't have been Crowley who'd found her because he would have left her dead. Someone wanted something. He was pretty sure she was still alive. But for how much longer? And what did that person want?

He couldn't lose her. She trusted him to keep her safe

and he let this happen. He'd let her down. She was probably huddled in a closet, fearing for her life. There had to be a way to find her, but he had no idea where to start. He ran a hand through his hair. He made fists at his sides and sucked in a breath. He needed a clear head to help Claire.

Chapter 17

Brad slammed closed the motel room door, raced to his truck as he pulled out his phone and dialed. "Mr. Purcell? It's Brad Hayes. I need your help."

He explained about Claire's disappearance and Purcell said he'd put his man, Thorndyke, on it.

He assumed whoever had taken Claire would head back home, so he started in that direction.

He'd driven a half-hour when his phone rang. He almost fumbled when he fished it from his pocket.

"Claire? Are you okay?" He yanked the wheel and stopped in the breakdown lane.

"Brad! This guy broke in. He's wearing a mask. He—"

"That's good enough. Now you know she's alive." There was no way to recognize the electronically altered voice, but it had to be Richards.

"What do you want?" Those few words from Claire offered a small amount of comfort. His fear and anger simmered under the surface.

"I'd like to do a little trade." There was no emotion in the altered voice. "You do what I want, and Claire goes free, unharmed."

"How do I know you'll let her go?"

"This is so complicated. It would be easier face to face, but that's not going to happen. I want you to confess to Captain Harkins about your gun running."

The man didn't answer Brad's question. He could do exactly what the man said and Claire could still die. His

121

anger flared and he suppressed it. It wouldn't help Claire. "Why should I confess to something I didn't do?" He took deep breaths, reminding himself he had to stay calm.

"Because it's going to save your girl. Crowley's been busy making sure the evidence implicates you. One bit of damning evidence is your dear friend didn't talk to you about his find." The man chuckled.

"It's not going to work." Brad gritted his teeth.

"It's all about perception. I know you've seen Dickens' evidence. You can give a convincing confession of how you ran the operation. Crowley will go down for the murder of his deputy. Of course, he won't make it to trial. Your girl will be proven innocent of murder. All you have to do to save her is confess."

"It would be more believable if I told him where I got the guns." Maybe he could get more information to pass on.

"You don't need to know. They'll think you're trying to protect your source. They won't look too close at a confession. Once you're booked, I'll let Claire go. Oh, and don't think you can recant your confession after Claire is free. There are many ways a person can die by accident."

His gut twisted. Would she always have this hanging over her?

"Harkins won't believe me."

"If someone else told him about you, he might not believe it. Why wouldn't he believe it from your own lips? Then the evidence will come in, proving it." He chuckled again. "You're screwed, Hayes, but Claire doesn't have to go down with you."

He let out a breath. "All right, give me the details." He'd do it and keep quiet. He'd go to prison if it meant Claire lived. Even if he didn't come out alive.

Brad tossed the phone on the seat and ran his hands through his hair, slammed them onto the steering wheel and roared. This was Jeffery's fault. Claire hadn't known anything until he wrenched her into it with a phone call. She almost died and was still in danger. He'd gotten desperate and not thought of the consequences.

Brad gripped the wheel, dropped his head against the headrest, and dragged in a slow breath and let it out. He needed to regain control to get this done.

Claire had said the man wore a mask. That was a good sign he intended on letting her go. Brad needed to do his part to save her.

Minutes after he got back on the road, his phone rang again. He didn't recognize the number. Was it Richards, calling from his own phone with more instructions? "Hayes."

"This is Thorndyke."

Purcell had mentioned that name.

"AG Purcell assigned me to monitor your phones. I got an earful."

"Thank God." Brad sighed. "I felt like I was all alone in this."

"Do you know who you were talking to?"

"I'm fairly sure it was Matt Richards."

"You're right. Agent Anderson was assigned to watch Richards. He saw him pick up Claire and followed them to a warehouse."

"He saw him kidnap Claire and didn't stop him?" She could be safe right now and they were playing games.

"We needed to get more on Richards."

"Attempted kidnapping would have been a good start." He worked at maintaining his control. These were supposed to be the good guys. He needed them.

"Yeah, well, he thought Richards would be picking up guns tonight. He wasn't prepared for what Richards did pick up."

"What are you going to do about this? You can't leave

her with him." If he'd been in Anderson's position, he'd have done whatever it took to prevent the kidnapping. At this point, Claire was all that mattered. He didn't care if Richards got way.

"We take Richards down and rescue Claire."

His heart constricted. Richards would be desperate. He wouldn't care if Claire got injured. How about the agents? Claire probably wouldn't be their priority. Sure, they would try to protect the civilian, but she wouldn't be as important to them as she was to him.

"I want in on it. I've had training in hostage situations."

"Let me get back to you on that. Give me a few." He hung up.

Brad pulled off the road again. He didn't know if he'd be going to the station or where ever Claire was. His fingers drummed on the steering wheel. He needed action. He snatched up his phone, jumped out of the truck and paced in front of it. They were wasting time. If he didn't get to the station soon enough, Richards would think he wasn't going to confess, and maybe hurt Claire. He checked his watch for the fifteenth time in as many minutes.

"Call, Thorndyke." Maybe they were rescuing Claire and taking down Richards as he sat in the middle of nowhere.

His heart pounded when his phone rang.

"We're meeting two blocks from their location." Thorndyke gave Brad the address.

Relief passed through him at being included. Brad punched it into his GPS and headed out. It should take forty minutes. He was sure he could shave off a lot of time.

Chapter 18

The masked man paced in front of Claire. She was tied to a rolling chair in the middle of an office, her wrists zip tied to the arms. A rope circled her waist, the back of the chair, her ankles and the center post, too tight for her feet to propel the chair. Not that there was anywhere to go.

The almost empty warehouse the man had led her through would offer no place to hide if she could get free. He'd locked the outside door with a key, so she'd still be trapped in the warehouse.

He said he'd let her go once Brad confessed, but she didn't trust him. She's read all the evidence Brad had. Two men already died in jail. Brad could become number three. Case closed after his confession and suicide. He risked everything for her.

They'd been so close to breaking the case, only to have the tables turned on them. She wouldn't see Brad again before she died. Her chest ached. Her stomach knotted. She blinked back tears and took a deep breath. No giving up.

Claire scrutinized the office again. Too bad her phone sat in the center of the farthest desk. If it was at the edge, she might have been able to scoot her chair over and snag it with her fingertips. Chances were slim she'd find a knife in the desk drawers. Pens and paperclips wouldn't do her much good.

"What are you waiting for?" Was that really her voice? It quavered like she was ninety. *Be strong.* That's all she had.

He faced her. His dark eyes glittered through the holes in

the mask. "I'm waiting for my inside guy to let me know Hayes has been booked."

She sucked in a breath. Then he'd kill her? Or wait until after they killed Brad? Maybe he told the truth and would let her go. Brad, being a cop, might not make it out of prison alive. Maybe that was their plan. "How long will it take?"

"As long as it takes!" The man stormed out of the office and out of sight.

She took a deep breath. *Okay. Don't rile up the guy with a gun.* Another breath. Maybe she should keep her mouth shut.

The man passed the door and a few moments later, passed again. Pacing. Maybe he was as nervous as her. If his plans fell apart, she'd be dead, and this man would go to prison. Was he an officer at the station? Or the special agent who broke into Jeffery's house? Maybe prison would be a death sentence for him.

At his first words, she held her breath. She didn't want to miss one syllable.

"Did Hayes get there yet?" After a pause, he said, "What? He should have been there ten minutes ago." Another pause. "Yeah, maybe. Give me a call when he gets there." He walked farther from the door. "I know it's not what we planned. I'm getting antsy. Just call me and call me again when he's booked." He paced closer to the door and away again.

A noise at the window distracted her. The room light revealed a face peering in. She didn't recognize him, but hoped he was there to rescue her. She nodded toward the door in hopes he would understand her kidnapper was out there. He nodded and disappeared. Claire turned back toward the door, not wanting to be caught staring at the window. She gripped the armrests to stop her hands from shaking.

That guy had to be there to rescue her. Who else would

peek in the window? Not someone just passing by. Not another bad guy. He must have a gun, but so did the guy inside. She was a lot closer to the bad guy. He could hold the gun to her head as soon as he heard anything suspicious.

She took deep breaths, and hoped she wouldn't die in a shootout.

****

Agent Thorndyke worked his way back to Brad and Anderson, where they waited behind a stockade fence at the edge of the property. "The woman is tied to a chair in the office."

"Her name is Claire." Brad needed to personalize her to make them be more careful.

Thorndyke glared at him. "Fine. Claire is alone, but she nodded toward the door. I assume Richards isn't far. The warehouse lights weren't on, so I couldn't see beyond the doorway. We don't know if it's full or empty."

"If it's empty," Brad said, "he'll see the door open and be back in the office in a flash with a gun to Claire's head."

Anderson pulled his gun and checked it. "I could stand at the window and shoot him when he comes in."

"We don't want him dead if we can help it," Thorndyke said.

"I can incapacitate him."

Brad's brows dropped. "I don't care if you kill him as long as Claire stays safe."

"She'll be fine. I'm good." Anderson's smug smile proved that, at least, he believed it.

Brad hoped he was justified. Claire's life depended on it. If Anderson didn't take Richards down, then Claire would become Richards' shield.

"Do you pick locks?" Brad asked Thorndyke.

"I've got my trusty little kit here." He patted his shirt pocket.

They ran to the corner of the building and waited as Anderson worked his way to the window. Brad and Thorndyke slipped around the corner to the door. Beside it were two commercial size garage doors. Brad stopped on the other side of the door, gripped his gun and held it up, ready to step in and point as soon as the door opened. Thorndyke worked his magic and nudged the door open.

Brad stepped through and scanned the space. A masked man stood in the office doorway. He made eye contact with Brad then stepped back into the office.

No! He could imagine Richards putting his gun to Claire's head. His heart twisted, and he raced for the office.

Two shots rang out.

"Claire!"

He stopped in the doorway. No thought to proper protocol, too panicked to care if Richards shot him.

He barely made note of Richards on the floor, blood on his knee and wrist.

Claire appeared unharmed. Beautiful but scared. Tears slipped down her cheeks.

"Brad!"

He wrapped his arms around her and kissed her forehead. "I'm so sorry I let this happen to you." He wiped away the tears. "Are you all right? Did he hurt you?

"I'm fine."

He pulled out his knife, cut through the bindings and gathered her into his arms. He'd been so afraid he'd never get to hold her again, the most precious person in the world.

Claire tipped back. "He talked to someone at the station. The man was going to call him when you got there."

Brad stilled. "There's someone else besides Crowley at the station?"

"I think so."

He turned to face the other men. "Guys, I have to go into the station and make that confession, after all."

Claire gasped and tightened her arms around him.

Both men gave him a puzzled stare.

"What?" Thorndyke asked.

"Claire said someone is supposed to call Richards when I get there. We need to find out who that is."

"All right," said Anderson. "I'll take him to the hospital." He nudged his foot into Richards' leg and the man grunted.

Richards sat on the floor, cradling a bloody hand. Blood pooled under his knee. His mask had been removed and lay beside him.

"I'll drop you at your truck, Hayes," said Thorndyke. "Then I'll take Claire to the motel to pick up your stuff and then drop her at her apartment. I'll take his phone with me." He pointed to Richards. "Once his contact calls, we'll arrest him, too. And Crowley."

Anderson put handcuffs on Richards and helped him up. They headed for the door.

****

Before Brad could open Thorndyke's car door, Claire clung to him. She'd been so worried about him and it wasn't over yet. She was safe now, so Brad could keep his full attention on saving himself. "Be careful. You don't know who to trust." She leaned back from him. "I want you back in one piece."

He kissed her. "I'll try my best."

He opened the door and turned back. "Hold on, I'll get your phone." He retrieved it, popped the battery in and powered it up.

129

"Here. You should be able to use your own now." He closed the door before she could respond.

Claire leaned between the seats. "Hey, Thorndyke, do you mind if I come up front? I feel like a prisoner back here by myself."

He chuckled. "Yeah, come on up."

They drove away as Brad held his phone to his ear.

She turned to Thorndyke. "Can you keep him safe?"

He flicked his head toward her and back to the road. "After I drop you off, I'm heading to the station. As soon as I get the call, I'm going in to arrest whoever it is."

Not a real answer, but the best she could expect.

They turned into the motel parking lot. Claire jumped out and stopped at the door when she remembered she didn't have a key.

Thorndyke stepped beside her. "Let me help with that." He pulled out his lock picks and had the door open in seconds.

"You've had a lot of practice, haven't you?"

"It comes in handy." He grinned. Bet he had some stories.

The smell of old Chinese food permeated the room. She dropped the bag in the trash can and peeked into the one beside it. Condoms. She rolled the top over and stuffed it into Brad's duffle, then gathered her belongings and was ready to leave in minutes.

They got into the car. "Would you mind dropping me at the cabin instead of my apartment? It's where my car is."

"No problem." Claire gave him directions and an uncomfortable hour later, he turned into the long driveway. Thorndyke checked everything out before letting her step inside and then instructed her to lock up before he left. Like that made much difference since people could pick locks. She shoved kitchen chairs under the doorknobs at front and back doors, and then sat on the couch and texted Brad to let him know where to find her.

Chapter 19

Before driving off, Brad called his captain. "Tom, sorry it's so late, but can you meet me at the station?"

Tom yawned. "Now?"

"If you wouldn't mind. It's important."

"All right. I'll be in ASAP."

When Brad walked into the station, he was surprised how many people were working at close to midnight. He stopped beside two people who were talking.

"What's up, Scott? Why so many people?" He waved to the room.

"There's a buzz that something's going down, but nobody seems to know what."

Brad frowned. Maybe someone wanted everybody to know about his confession.

Terry turned. "Hey, man. Do you know something?"

"Sorry, guys. Later." Brad walked back to Tom's office.

When he stepped through the door, Tom slipped his cell phone back into his pocket. Brad paused as a shiver wound up his spine. It may have been a coincidence. No way was Tom a part of this gun running business. Brad took a few more steps and dropped into one of the chairs in front of Tom's desk.

Tom leaned back. "What's this all about, Brad? It's been a long time since I got called in at midnight."

"Well, I thought you might like to be the one to hear a confession."

Tom lifted one eyebrow. "Whose confession?"

Brad wondered if Tom had feigned innocence. He didn't want to believe a man he'd come to respect would let Brad go down for something he hadn't done.

He had no idea how long it would take for Thorndyke to get in and arrest the guy on the other end of the cell phone. It would probably be at least a half hour. He didn't want to actually confess to gun running, even if he could walk it back. "Maybe mine. Should we record this?" Setting it up should take some time.

"Maybe you should tell me whatever it is and I'll decide if we need to make a recording."

Brad rubbed his hand down his face. He needed to stall.

He almost told Tom he'd found Claire, but if Tom was the inside contact, then he'd know they'd taken out Richards.

"You know Claire didn't kill Jeffery."

"Why would I know that?"

"Maybe you wouldn't," unless he was working with Crowley, "but I do. Claire grew up with Jeffery and me. The three of us were inseparable from kindergarten to high school graduation."

Tom raised his eyebrows. He must not have known.

Brad nodded. "So, even though Claire divorced Jeffery, she still cared too much to harm him."

Tom leaned forward. "Given the right provocation, anyone can kill."

Brad gave a quick nod. "True. I think Claire could kill with the right provocation. But this wasn't it, and she would never kill Jeffery." She *had* shot the sheriff. If she hadn't been so rushed, it could have been a kill. Even after Jeffery's murder was resolved, she might have been charged.

Tom rested his palms on the desk. "This doesn't sound like a confession."

Brad shrugged and smirked. "What can I say? I'm not good at confessions."

Tom's hands closed into fists. "You woke me up for this? We could have had this discussion in the morning."

"It is kind of late." Brad stood. "Do you want a cup of coffee? I could sure use some."

"What?" Tom fell back in his chair. "Fine. I'll have two sugars."

At the coffee station, Brad was relieved the pot was almost empty. He dumped out the dregs and started a fresh pot. Two bonuses, fresh coffee and a delay in his confession. He took two Styrofoam cups off the stack. At least he hadn't been hauled into an interview room where he might not have been given a glass of water.

Maybe it was a good thing Tom didn't want to record yet. He didn't want anything sounding like a confession recorded before an arrest was made.

When the coffee machine stopped gurgling, he lifted the pot and filled the cups, adding sugar to the captains.

Back in the office, he set one cup on the desk and took a sip of the other, then settled into his chair. He took another drink, waiting for Tom to say something.

The captain took a gulp from his cup. "Now, are you making a confession?"

"You want me to tell you how I've been procuring guns and selling them to gangs and survivalists?"

"If that's what you want to tell me." Tom sat back in his chair, crossed his arms, his face grim.

Brad stared at him. Tom didn't seem surprised Brad was confessing to gunrunning. He didn't want the man to find that believable. Maybe he'd been informed of Brad's reason for being there. It turned out Brad didn't know Tom after all. They'd worked together for four years and he never once thought Tom would do anything illegal.

"All right," Brad stretched out the words. "Where should I begin?"

"When did it start?"

"About three years ago."

"Who else is in it?"

"Dean Crowley." He'd take Crowley down even if he had to go with him, but he hoped he didn't.

"Anyone else?"

Brad shrugged. He couldn't mention Matt Richards. "Small guys."

The door flew open and crashed against the wall. Brad turned in his chair to see Thornkyke standing in the doorway. "You're under arrest."

Brad stood. For a second, he thought Thorndyke was going to arrest him.

Thorndyke walked past him and stopped beside Tom. "Stand up, Harkins."

"What? Who the hell are you? You should be arresting Hayes."

Brad put his hands on his hips, a small smile flickered across his face.

Thorndyke grabbed Tom's upper arm, yanked him up, dragged Tom's hands behind his back and cuffed him. He turned to Brad. "Richards' call routed through the station's switchboard, but Harkin used his own cell to tell Richards you'd gotten to the station."

Brad nodded. He was dazed his boss was one of the bad guys. It had begun to dawn on him while they were talking, but it still seemed unreal.

"I've got a couple guys on their way over to the sheriff's house to take him in, too."

Brad nodded again. Was it finally over? "Thanks, Thorndyke."

As Thornkyke passed with Tom, he leaned close. "I left Claire at a cabin because she wanted to be dropped where her car was."

"Thanks." Brad wasn't sure if Claire had stayed at the cabin or driven herself home. Her apartment was a few blocks from the station, so he'd drive by there first.

After he climbed into his truck, he checked his phones and found the text from Claire. She was at the cabin and would wait up for him. Soon, she'd be in his arms.

Chapter 20

As Brad raced up the long driveway to the cabin, the light in the window called to him, showing she was still awake, waiting for him. Why had she decided to stay at the cabin? He rounded the house and parked beside her car. He got out and noticed the curtain drop closed, then the door opened and Claire flew down the steps and into his arms.

He spun in a circle. He'd almost lost her and for a while, he thought he'd never have the chance to hold her again. "I was so scared when I found you gone. I would have made that confession if I hadn't already talked to the Attorney General."

Claire gazed up at him, tears glistening. "Brad—"

He put his fingers over her mouth. "It's over." He kissed her, then raised his head. "Are you okay? It was so hard to leave you earlier. I didn't get a chance to make sure you weren't hurt."

She nibbled his lips. "I'm fine now that you're back. He didn't hurt me, but I was scared for both of us."

He tightened his arms around her, then scooped her up. "Let's go in and I'll show you how much I missed you."

He let his shoulders relax as he reminded himself Claire was safe. She peered up at him with merriment in her eyes. He smiled in return and couldn't resist another kiss. He passed through the open door and kicked it shut.

He paused before stepping into the bedroom. In all the years he'd come to this cabin, he'd never set foot in this room. When they were growing up, it was Derrick's and off limits. Later, when he and Jeffery had come, Jeffery had used it.

He stepped through, registering his bag from the motel sitting on the floor, the box of condoms sitting on the nightstand and the bed covers pulled back. Her thoughts were exactly where his were.

At the bed, he let her slide down his body. He raced to unbutton his shirt, watching as Claire did the same with the shirt she wore.

His shirt slid off his shoulders just as hers did. She was naked and beautiful. A sight he wanted to see every night and morning. He took her hands in his and kissed each one as he stared into her soft, brown eyes. He almost forgot what he was going to say.

He glanced at the bed. This time would be different. They weren't two desperate people on the run. She was special. The most important person in the world.

"I love you, Claire. I wanted you to know before we made love again."

She stretched up and kissed him. "I love you, too. Now can you finish undressing?"

He half smiled. He liked how impatient she was. "Not yet. This was Derrick's room."

Claire frowned, but gave a nod.

"I feel we should honor him by at least being engaged before making love in here."

Her mouth dropped open. She leaned back. "Are you asking me to marry you?"

He lifted an eyebrow. "I guess I didn't do that very well." As he sunk to his knees, he kissed each breast and her abdomen. One knee on the floor, his gaze on her beautiful glistening eyes, he kissed her hands. They trembled. "Claire, I've loved you my entire life. I would be honored and elated if you would marry me."

She drew her hands back, and for a second, he thought she'd refuse. His heart plummeted to his stomach. But, she slid down in front of him, giving him time to kiss each breast. Once on her knees, she wrapped her arms around his neck. His heart soared.

"I can't imagine anything I would love more than to be your wife." She kissed him. "Yes, I'll marry you."

She pressed against him and he ground into her. She was always his dream wife. No one else had ever been good enough. His heart would burst with the love he could finally show her. Every day, she'd know how important she was, how much love he had to give her.

She laughed when he surged up, with her still in his arms. He lowered her to the bed, then finished undressing. Putting a hand on each side of her head, he kissed her. He slid into the bed and tugged her on top of him. Her warmth flowed into all the spaces that had been empty for so long. Her quick kisses were a tease. He growled, threaded his fingers through her hair, and deepened the kiss. The other hand slid down her back, crushing her to the evidence of his desire. His thoughts centered on how he would please his fiancée.

Chapter 21

Claire stretched beside Brad. Light filtered through his eyelids. It had to still be early. She started to scoot out of bed but he looped his arm around her and tucked her back in. "Mmm. Don't leave yet. You feel so good next to me."

He opened his eyes and glanced at the clock. A little after nine. They must have gotten about four hours of sleep, but he felt wonderful.

She twisted around and smiled, wrapped her arm over his shoulder and kissed him.

Even with so little sleep, she was beautiful. The haunted expression was gone.

She nibbled his ear. "Since I'm awake and you're awake and you don't want me to leave…"

He slid his hand up her back, tangled it in her hair and found her lips. "I like waking up like this." Her kisses made his blood boil.

A phone trilled. He frowned and dropped his head onto the pillow. Almost the worst time for an interruption. "That sounds like mine." He scrambled to the end of the bed, and fished his phone out of his pants pocket. "Hayes."

"This is Thorndyke. I was wondering if you and your lady could come into your station about one today so we can wrap things up."

He turned his head toward Claire. "I think we can manage that. And, Thorndyke, I owe you big time. Thanks."

"We're even on this one." He hung up.

They were nowhere near even. Thorndyke captured

three criminals, but the woman Brad loved was alive and was his.

Brad dropped his phone onto his pants and sat up.

Claire had wrapped her arms around her drawn up knees. He gave her knee a squeeze. "Do you want to stay in bed longer?" He wiggled his eyebrows. "Or shall I cook breakfast?"

She laughed. "Who needs to eat?"

****

Brad held Claire's hand as they walked into the station. Her hand tightened in his and he glanced back at her. She caught her lip between her teeth.

All eyes followed them, and no one said a word as they stepped into the large room. It must have been a shock to find out what Crowley and Harkins had done. He waved and lengthened his stride.

She huffed out a breath when they stepped into Brad's office and he shoved the door closed.

"Everybody was staring at me. They still think I killed Jeffery."

"No. They were staring at us being together. I've never brought a woman into the station. They think I've got a great catch." He smiled and kissed her.

She shook her head. "More likely, they're wondering why you're with Jeffery's ex-wife."

"They'll find out soon enough." He pointed at the couch. "Why don't you have a seat while I go find Thorndyke?"

He waited for her to get comfortable, then closed the door behind him. On his way to the conference room, he stopped at the voices in one of the interrogation rooms. He slipped into the neighboring room to watch through the two-way mirror.

Thorndyke sat at the table across from another man Brad didn't know. He was about thirty, with short, dark hair. He seemed a little nervous, but no more than anybody would be in this situation. As the questioning continued, Brad realized this man ran the evidence room of the station Jason Miller had worked in.

"How did the guns disappear?" Thorndyke asked.

"I don't know. I'm not the only one who mans that room."

Thorndyke opened a folder in front of him and extracted a sheet of paper. Text was highlighted in light green on the page. Thorndyke dropped the paper in front of the other man.

"You were working when Matt Richards signed in." Thorndyke pointed at the highlighted line. Brad leaned closer to the glass and stared at the man. Matt had been in the evidence room?

The man's gaze darted to the page and back to Thorndyke. "Okay, what about it?"

"Did he only check evidence on the murder indicated here?" Thorndyke stabbed his finger at a spot on the page.

"I don't know," mumbled the man.

"How did you not know? Didn't you get it for him?"

"Um." The man stared at his hands.

"Did he get it himself?" Thorndyke asked, louder.

Still staring at his hands, the man said, "He told me to take a break and I left."

"You left your post?" Thorndyke's control teetered.

The man straightened and stared at Thorndyke. "It's not like he's a criminal. He's from the state attorney's office."

"And didn't it seem a little out of the ordinary for him to tell you to leave?"

"Yeah, but he's from the state attorney's office." The man's voice became desperate.

Thorndyke jabbed a finger at his own chest. "I'm from

the state attorney's office. I wouldn't ask you to leave your post. Did you go to your captain and telling him about it?"

"Um, no." He mumbled.

"How long were you gone?"

"About ten minutes."

"Was Richards still there when you got back?"

"No."

Thorndyke sat back and studied the man. "This is going on your record. I'll leave your pending employment up to your captain. You can leave."

Brad waited until the man exited the room and passed his door before he stepped into the hallway and entered the interrogation room.

"Afternoon, Thorndyke."

Thorndyke glanced up at Brad and the barest of smiles showed on his lips and was gone. "We've been busy since last I saw you. Crowley's been arrested. He and Harkins have both lawyered up, so we haven't gotten much out of either of them."

Brad nodded. "Claire's in my office. She should be able to give you more ammo against Crowley."

"Good, and the men who were with Richards are turning on him for a lighter sentence. We've also placed him in the station the night the gunrunner, Edward Cunningham, died. We'll tie it to him somehow." He stood. "Let's go talk to Claire. How is she holding up?"

"Amazingly well. She wants to make sure Crowley goes down for Jeffery's murder." He did, too. He'd lost his best friend and Claire had come close to dying because of Crowley. He led the way to his office.

As Brad opened his door, he said, "Do you think—" Claire lay asleep on the couch, her bare feet tucked under her, and her head on his rolled up jacket. He smiled at her disorientation as her eyes fluttered open.

"Oh, sorry. I fell asleep." She sat up and slipped her feet into her shoes.

Thorndyke stepped closer. "That's all right, Claire. You had an exhausting day yesterday. Why don't I get coffee for the three of us while you finish waking up?"

Claire nodded and rubbed her eyes.

After Thorndyke left, Brad squatted in front of her. "I shouldn't have kept you up so late last night."

She cupped his face with her hands. "I wouldn't have missed it for the world. It's not every day a woman gets proposed to."

Thorndyke waltzed in, juggling three cups. "Why don't we sit at the desk?"

He sat the cups in the center of it. "You two sit there." He pointed to the two chairs in front of the desk as he sat in Brad's chair. He pulled a small recorder from his shirt pocket and poked a button. "This is Ralph Thorndyke interviewing Claire Dickens concerning the shooting death of Deputy Jeffery Dickens and shooting injury of Sheriff Dean Crowley. Some comments may be added by Officer Brad Hayes."

For the next hour, they worked through the details of the night Jeffery died. Brad had never asked Claire for specifics, not wanting to upset her. As she described the events of that night, her voice quivered. He took her hand and she glanced at him, tears shimmering in her eyes. They'd lost a dear friend that night.

They continued with where and when Brad found the evidence Jeffery had acquired and finished with Claire's abduction and rescue.

Thorndyke leaned forward. "Now, about this witness."

Brad glanced at Claire. "She's Candy Pruitt, a waitress at *Captain's Net*. She was taking a break on a bench in front of the restaurant when Jeffery was shot. I'm not telling where she is until it's guaranteed Crowley is not getting out on bail."

"Agreed. But we're going to call her so I can get her statement."

Brad held up his prepaid phone. "If we call her from this phone."

Thorndyke nodded.

Brad dialed and waited for her to pick up. Once she answered, Brad put the call on speaker. Thorndyke walked her through the interview, his voice gentle. Candy's voice shook as she relived the terrifying scene.

Brad told her to stay away until he notified her it was safe, then pocketed his phone.

Thorndyke smiled at Claire. "This tentatively clears you of wrongdoing. I've already voided the arrest warrant." He stood. "Your station now has three job openings. I'm sure you can have your pick. I know Attorney General Purcell will give you a recommendation." He held out his hand. "It's been a pleasure working with you."

Brad shook it. "Same here."

Claire held out her hand. "Thank you for saving my life."

Thorndyke took it. "It was a group effort, Claire, but you're welcome." He gave them a mock salute and left.

She turned to Brad, her shoulders relaxed. A real smile warmed her features. "I would love to curl up in a bed somewhere with you. Do you have to stay?"

His breath hitched. Would she always have this affect on him? "No, let's get out of here. Your place or mine?"

"Mmm. Yours."

****

When they reached Brad's truck, her phone rang. She

hadn't heard it in over a week. She glanced at Brad before checking it. It was her editor. She'd seen a couple messages from him, but hadn't listened to them yet. Brad helped her into the truck as she answered.

"Hi, Jacob. What's up?" Luckily, she'd been between assignments when she had to disappear.

"Claire, it's wonderful to talk to you. I hear you've been cleared of murdering your husband. Congratulations." He almost always sounded cheery.

"What? How did you hear that already?" There was no way he could know.

"Oh, I have my connections. I called to give you an assignment."

"Already? I don't know if I'm ready."

"I think you can handle it. I'd like an exclusive on your brush with the law and tracking down the dirty cops."

"Sometimes you scare me, Jacob. How do you know all this?"

He chuckled. "I'll never tell. How soon do you think you can have something for me?"

She stared at Brad. "Give me a chance to organize something and I'll let you know."

"Okay. Glad to hear your voice, Clairy. Talk to you in a couple days."

"Bye, Jacob."

Brad lifted his brows.

"My editor wants me to write up the story."

He nodded. "Can you run it by me before you submit it?"

"Sure. But if you want me to make changes, you better have good reasons."

"Only the best."

He leaned across the seat and kissed her. "I can't get enough of you."

Epilogue

Claire gazed around Brad's bedroom. Their bedroom. She'd given up her apartment, and moved into his house. It still needed work, but he'd decorated this room the same way he had at his last house, using the colors of paint and carpeting she'd suggested back then.

They'd had to merge three households of furniture, but ended up with a nice mix throughout. She'd sold Jeffery's house to a police officer, and left some of the furniture for his family, including leaving the man cave intact.

She clamored from the bed, the full-length mirror on the closet door catching her eye. She stood naked, her shoulder toward the glass, her fingertips touching her stomach. It was almost too good to be true. Three months ago, she wouldn't have believed she would be loved by the most wonderful man in the world and they would soon have a baby. Surviving those couple of weeks had seemed impossible, but during that time, they'd created a new life.

A comb dropped onto the bathroom counter. Brad walked up behind her, wrapped one arm under her breasts and smoothed his other hand over her stomach. She snuggled back into his bare chest.

Her gaze met his in the mirror. "Do you think anyone can tell I'm pregnant yet?"

He kissed her neck. "Only me." He rubbed circles over her almost flat belly.

She stared at his hand and threaded her fingers through his. "I don't want to look pregnant in my wedding dress."

"It's only next week. You'll be beautiful."

She spun and kissed his bare chest then smiled up at him. "Thank you for asking Jeffery's father to walk me down the aisle. I was so afraid he and Ann hated me." She'd hated herself for a while after she'd found out Jeffery hadn't cheated. His parents had reason to hate her.

He gave her a quick kiss. "They don't. I explained everything to them. They never blamed you. And they asked me to bring you for dinner next Wednesday."

She bit her lip. "Um, okay." It sounded like everything would be fine, and she liked Jeffery's parents. She always had. Sometimes when she was young, she wished they were her parents.

"It'll be fine. Shall we tell them about the baby then?"

Her heart stuttered. "I don't know how they'll feel about it. They knew Jeffery and I were trying to have a baby."

"Honey, they love you. They want you to be happy. Growing up, you were a fixture at their house as much as me. They'll be happy for you. For us."

She nodded. "You're right. Let's tell them."

She sighed. At that very moment, her life was perfect. She was days from marrying the man she loved, who loved her as much. They were having a baby. Her in-laws were still family. She'd never been able to think of them as ex-in-laws.

It still hurt that she'd believed lies about Jeffery and never got the chance to ask him to forgive her. She closed her eyes. *Jeffery, I hope you can hear me. Forgive me for not believing you. If I had, we could have spent those last months together. I'm sorry.* Peace enveloped her like a hug and tears trickled down her cheeks.

Brad lifted her chin. "Hey, what's this?"

She smiled. "I think Jeffery forgave me."

"He never blamed you."

"I know, but I think I had to forgive myself, too."

148

His arms tightened around her. "I love you, and if I didn't have to get to work, you'd know how much."

She grinned. "Oh, I know how much." She wiggled her hips.

He stepped away from her, and pulled on his pants. He took a tan shirt off a hanger and pinned on his badge, turning as he slipped his arms into the sleeves.

She stopped in front of him and buttoned the first button, then the second. On the third, she said, "This is more fun doing the opposite."

He chuckled. "I'll give you that chance tonight."

She stood on her toes and kissed him. "You better, Sheriff."

THE END

Books by Deborah Wallace

Rawlins Series
Kathleen's Legacy
Forbidden Woman
Jamie's Trials
Adam's Redemption
Kristy's Puzzle – *Winter 2020*

Wounded Warrior Hearts Series
Wounded Warrior Hearts: Steven
Wounded Warrior Hearts: Amy
Wounded Warrior Hearts: Russ

Other Books
Second Choice
I Shot the Sheriff
Only My Love
New Memories

Check out my website for details on these books and where to find them. You can also sign up to receive emails when I have a new book. www.DeborahWallaceBooks.com.

About Deborah Wallace

Someone suggested I try writing, and stories started populating my brain, begging to be put on paper (or my computer screen).

I have been called a Jane-of-all-trades, from seamstress to house and furniture designer/builder to computer programmer to technical writer and bookkeeper. I even do car maintenance. I've also guided a team of 'Future Problem Solvers'.

I grew up in Michigan, but Massachusetts has been my home for more years than I care to think about. I love the history here, the museums and antique houses, the seacoast and hiking trails.

My three children have grown and scattered, but my husband is by my side, encouraging my writing.

www.ingramcontent.com/pod-product-compliance
Lightning Source LLC
Chambersburg PA
CBHW022019170626
46808CB00003B/986